The Patriot and the Antifa

A Love Story

C. Lexcourt

C. Lexcourt Imprints

This is a work of fiction. Names, characters, organizations, places, events, and incidents either are the product of the author's imagination or are used fictitiously. Any resemblance to actual persons, living or dead, or actual events is purely coincidental.

This book contains explicit sexual content and depictions of political violence. It is intended for mature readers.

Cover illustration by Georgette Meadofoam

ISBNs
Hardcover: 979-8-9944573-2-0
Paperback: 979-8-9944573-1-3
Ebook: 979-8-9944573-3-7

Published by C. Lexcourt Imprints

First edition, 2026

Printed in the United States of America

Contents

PART ONE

1

Beefwell

Protein powder, an upstart crypto trading platform, and dick pills he definitely didn't need—after two years of grinding, Chet Beefwell finally had three solid sponsors. Not bad for a guy who recorded his podcast at a desk in the corner of his living room. One mic, no intro music; just the sound of his voice echoing against the blank walls.

"Welcome back to *Ripped for the Right*," he said. "Today I want to talk about pressure: Internal. External. Cultural..." He paused and stared into the distance as if there was a camera on him. There wasn't—not yet—but it would have looked sick.

He was recording earlier than usual today. The Antifa goons were planning to riot and spread chaos in the streets again. As always, he would be there to stand up to them. If there was one thing Chet couldn't stand, it was a bully.

"We live in a time where the body is seen as trivial," he continued, "but it isn't. The body is where our strength lives. And strength? It's about stewardship."

He liked the sound of that for a day like today. The guys in the group chat said turnout was going to be big. The Soros brain virus was spreading; more and more of these thugs were showing up, which meant things got dicier faster.

"A lot of people out there want to erode our bodies. Erode our minds. Erode our freedoms. But erosion can only happen when you're not making your move." He gazed around the room, nodding to himself, thinking of the black-clad mobs he would encounter downtown, too chickenshit to show their faces.

Chet slammed his fist on the desk. "I'm not gonna erode. I'm gonna remember. I'm gonna move. And I'm gonna push back!"

At the thirty-minute mark, he wrapped the episode. He saved the file then lowered himself to the cold floor to do three sets of twelve push-ups. Each descent was steady—inhale, pause at the bottom, rise. The point wasn't exhaustion. It was control.

When he stood, his right knee throbbed—football injury, junior year. It had been acting up lately, but he would manage.

He drank two full glasses of water at the sink. His grandmother taught him to start every day like that. She'd passed a few years ago but lived on in little rules like that—water before coffee, eat slowly and with intention, look a person in the eye when you're talking to them. She never used words like "mindful." Just said, "Don't be in such a damn rush."

Green Henley. Blue jeans. Shoes he could kick someone with if needed. He stood for a moment, staring himself down in the mirror.

Before he left, Chet cracked three eggs into a mason jar and drank them raw. The glass had a faint chip in the rim and a World Market sticker still clinging to the base. His ex had picked it out. Chet used to laugh at Anna for drinking out of jars. Then he started doing it himself. Now she lived in Austin and sold ashtrays shaped like hands.

Last time they spoke, she told him she was dating a woman named Joy. "She's a DJ," Anna said, "and a nutritionist." Then she'd paused, as if waiting for him to tell her he'd changed, too.

He set the jar in the sink and grabbed his keys.

Outside, the bushes swayed like boxers getting ready to land their first punch. As Chet got into his Tacoma, he felt something curled low in his stomach. Not fear, more like the sense that something had already started, and he was just catching up to it.

2

Soyvenus

Jennifer Soyvenus was just about to come when the sound of Marnie grinding coffee beans in the kitchen intruded like a riot cop charging a mostly-peaceful crowd of protesters.

Sighing, she tossed her vibrator aside and checked her phone. 7:23 a.m. Later than she wanted, but she would still make it to the protest on time.

She had packed her medic kit the night before. It was stuffed with gloves, bandages, eyewash, and snack bars. She considered bringing her pepper spray; Marnie had insisted she start carrying it after an incident a few months ago. A right-winger kicked her in the ribs while she was kneeling to treat a protester. Instead, she added a second bottle of eyewash.

Jennifer worked as a nurse at a private Catholic hospital across town. This allowed her to live comfortably enough without accepting money from her parents. It also gave her access to medical supplies, as long as she only took a few items at a time to avoid detection—a box of gloves here, a few rolls of gauze there.

In the kitchen, Marnie was making pour-over and humming something tuneless. She wore a blanket over her shoulders and had a cigarette tucked behind one ear. "Morning," she said. "Coffee?"

"Is it conflict-free?" Jennifer asked.

Marnie didn't look up. "Is anything?"

They both giggled.

Marnie rummaged in the junk drawer for a lighter. "I'll be back."

"At least eat first," Jennifer said. She grabbed two yogurts from the fridge and handed one to Marnie. Then she fished a clean-enough mug from the drying rack and poured a cup.

At the kitchen table, she opened her journal. Inside were small, all-caps entries from the last few days:

MAKE SPACE FOR GRIEF (ALSO BLOATING?)

WE ALL CONTRIBUTE IN DIFFERENT WAYS

NO MORE IDEALIZING "HEALTHY BOUNDARIES" GUYS WHO WEAR RINGS

She flipped to a blank page and considered her affirmation for the day. She'd felt more anxious before protests recently. Still, she'd been a protest medic since college and refused to stop doing her part. As scary as they might get for her, she knew it was nothing compared to the horrors immigrants and people of color faced every day under the rise of American fascism. She wasn't the kind of person who could sit by and let injustice happen.

She wrote:

LOVE MEANS ACTION.

Marnie dragged a stool over and set her mug on the table, scrolling TikTok. "Ready?" she asked.

"Yeah," Jennifer replied. "You change your mind about coming?"

Marnie shook her head. "Too many nutjobs. I'll repost."

Jennifer pursed her lips but didn't say anything. She and Marnie became friends through activism in college. They had bonded over their commitment to the cause. Recently though, as street clashes with the alt-right heated up, Marnie had amped up her rhetoric yet become more hesitant to actually show up.

Jennifer finished her coffee and went back to her room to get dressed—black jeans with a small bleach stain, black hoodie, no logos.

She was pulling on her Doc Martens when Dev called. For a second, she considered letting it go to voicemail, but answered on the fourth ring.

"Hey."

"Babe," Dev said. "Are you still going or...?"

"Yeah, of course. Heading out now."

Dev sucked his teeth. "I was totally excited to go, but I didn't sleep at all. The neighbors were partying until like four last night and I don't want to impact the vibe."

Jennifer rubbed her temple. "Feel better, okay? I'll check in later."

There was a long pause. Then Dev said, "I'll be thinking about you," and hung up before she could respond.

On the bus, Jennifer closed her eyes and pictured the layout of the protest. Something about the buzz of it enthralled her—the crush of bodies, the signs, the rhythm of chants. The clarity she felt in a space where nothing else existed but hope and rage.

Her phone buzzed once. A message from Dev: *Don't get arrested unless it's sexy.*

She didn't respond.

3

Tear Gas and Thigh Contact

Buses arrived in scattered waves from uptown and the suburbs. Traffic was jammed for blocks, with cars missing their turns then looping through nearby neighborhoods.

Jennifer and her crew showed up on time but ended up on the wrong side of the square. Blocks from the protest, they were already encountering riot vans parked with half-geared cops lounging on nearby curbs, some still finishing sandwiches. They always staged themselves closer to the right-wingers before these things.

Jennifer walked a few paces ahead of the others, hoodie up, sunglasses on.

Leah trailed behind, followed by Katie and Mark. "We went the exact wrong way," Leah said, unaware of how loud she was being in enemy territory. "We'll be flanked by chuds before we even reach our comrades."

Leah was newer to the scene, brasher. It was her first year teaching at a local elementary school, and she was young and full of idealistic urgency. Like many new activists, she tended to think more in slogans than tactics. Still, Jennifer reminded herself, it was good more people were showing up. She just wished they'd get it together a bit faster.

"It'll be fine," said Jennifer. "The show hasn't started yet."

"This isn't a show," said Leah. "These are dangerous people."

Katie and Mark exchanged glances.

When they reached the plaza, Leah shot Jennifer a look. They were in a sea of American and Blue Lives Matter flags. Somebody nearby waved a handmade Pepe the Frog sign.

Then—a shoulder bump. Hard enough to jolt her, soft enough to be an accident.

"Watch it," came a voice.

Jennifer looked up. A tall guy in a green Henley had his hand up. He was flanked by two other gym bros—one short and twitchy, the other broad and bearded. All three wore mirrored aviator sunglasses, like a military-themed boy band.

Jennifer's throat clenched. She stepped sideways, head down. "Sorry."

The group beelined to their side of the plaza.

Chet watched her go. She was pretty with a soft mouth and sharp shoulders. Her big, deep-blue eyes, like the corner of the American flag, twinkled like stars. A deceptively tempting Antifa succubus. It was sad when the pretty ones got brainwashed.

She had looked at him like he was the edge of a cliff.

Jax spat loudly and cracked his knuckles like a man warming up for a cage match. "No one seems especially angry," he said, glancing down at the GoPro strapped to his chest. "I thought there'd be more energy."

"It's early," Chet said. They stood quietly for a moment, watching a group of black-clad freaks begin an unintelligible chant. "Sometimes I wonder if there's a way to bring them back to their senses."

Tyler scoffed. "Dream on."

A cop approached. He was older with careful posture and solid pecs. He stopped a few feet away and greeted them with a nod. "Appreciate you all staying peaceful today," he said.

"Of course," Chet replied. "We're just here to protect you from the Soros mob."

The officer hesitated, lips tightening. "Okay. Well—let's all just do our best not to escalate."

"Understood," Chet said, hands visible, palms relaxed. He meant it. He was a peaceful warrior. A small plug in the dam holding back the rising tide of left-wing chaos.

The officer flashed a thumbs up and walked away.

Jax gave a low whistle. "They used to be cooler. Police these days are starting to act all cucked."

Chet didn't respond.

The crowd across the plaza was growing. A sprawl of patchwork banners, rainbow umbrellas, and mutual aid tables. Someone handed out free Narcan kits beside a makeshift altar of fake candles and laminated flyers of left-wing martyrs.

"These pussies." Jax shook his head. "One shove and they'd all scatter like roaches."

"Well, that's exactly the problem," Tyler said. "We let *them* start shit. If we jump first, it's gonna look bad on the stream."

"They'll start something anyway," Chet added. "We're just here to stand our ground."

Leah was standing on a milk crate again, barking orders at no one in particular like she was auditioning for a role as a guerrilla general. "We need people west of the canopy. And I need two peace marshals over here *now—*"

Jennifer rolled her eyes and leaned toward Mark. "Should someone give her a megaphone?"

Mark laughed nervously but didn't answer.

"Jennifer, are you signed up for anything?" Leah called from her stage.

Jennifer flashed her a thumbs up. "Tear gas treatment. Like always, babe. I think we're set."

Energy was building. The drum circle had started, and a guy in a giant paper mache Che Guevara head danced through the crowd. A group of black blockers nearby was already arguing with an older man in a tie-dye shirt.

Meanwhile, Chet and his crew were forming up like a football team. Tyler checked the livestream chat on his phone. Jax kept egging people on, catcalling anyone in black. "Come show me your face, pussy!" and "Come get ratioed in real life, bitch!"

A line of volunteer peace marshals tried to wedge themselves between the two sides, but it wasn't working. The cops remained visible but largely removed from the action—typical, letting the tension simmer until someone snapped.

Chants rose in various pockets of the crowd, then died. Jennifer considered joining one, but decided to save her energy. She looked around, reading some signs. All the typical slogans.

Then someone screamed. It wasn't big, but enough to turn heads.

A glass bottle shattered near someone's foot.

"WHO FUCKING THREW THAT?"

The yelling started small, then erupted.

Jennifer spotted a guy in a tactical vest ripping off someone's mask.

A black flag whipped through the air like a threat.

"They need us at the front," Jennifer said. "We need bodies up there."

Leah was watching the scene with fear in her eyes. "Let's hang back 'til we get a sense of what's happening."

"I came here to do something." Jennifer turned and headed toward the action.

"Back the fuck up!" a marshal shouted. No one listened.

Chet's crew became increasingly agitated as the scene unfolded. Jax was live, panning the chaos. His chest-cam caught someone swinging a megaphone.

Someone misted the crowd with bear mace. Both sides surged forward. Punches flew. People screamed. Water bottles turned into projectiles.

Chet moved toward the center—instinct more than decision—faster than Tyler and Jax could follow through the mass.

A guy wearing raccoon ears climbed someone's shoulders, pelting the crowd with glitter bombs. Jennifer ducked and stumbled backward.

Her friends were pushing forward to join her, Leah bringing up the rear.

An open can of Zyn arced through the air, raining pouches on the crowd.

Cops barked warnings through megaphones.

Chet pushed past a guy in rollerblades and ducked past someone holding a handmade sign.

The knee came fast—a blur before impact, direct and unforgiving. Chet doubled over, one hand clutching his crotch, the other grasping at nothing. His stomach churned like that time he'd eaten something with cumin in it.

When he looked up, there she was again—the Antifa succubus. His eyes flicked over her. Black shirt. Jeans hugging her thighs for dear life.

"Get back," Jennifer said. "We don't want you here."

Chet hesitated.

"I said get back!"

"That was unprovoked," he said.

"You were moving toward people who didn't provoke you."

"I was trying to—"

Neither noticed the cops closing in on them until nylon cinched around their wrists.

Jennifer exhaled, adrenaline snapping through her limbs like static, as the cops pulled her backward. The zip tie sharply bit into the skin of her wrist.

They pushed her to the curb. She barely caught herself from falling fully sideways.

Next to her, the red-pill guy shouted out as he hit the concrete. His thigh collided with hers—warm, solid muscle under rough denim. The contact was brief but electric, like a strike-anywhere match scraping against a rock in some post-apocalyptic forest.

"Perfect," she muttered.

He turned slightly toward her, his breath catching in his throat like he hadn't expected her voice to be that close. "I didn't come here to fight," he said. "That's your guys' M.O."

Jennifer tilted her chin toward him defiantly. "You just brought backup and coordinated outfits."

"Says the lady in the Soros-issued, all-black uniform."

Jennifer snorted, almost charmed. His comeback was more clever than she would expect from a bonehead.

The shouting nearby had dulled to background noise—megaphone static, sirens, some woman crying with theatrical flair. A protest medic passed and offered them water from a cracked Nalgene, but neither of them moved.

She could smell him now—faint salt, cheap deodorant, maybe leather? Unironically masculine.

His shoulder knocked lightly against hers.

Their bodies were magnetic, suspended in the awkwardness of forced proximity—an unspoken battle for space and control.

"Well, I guess you won't get to set any fires today, princess. Sorry."

Wow, this guy liked to spar. Up close, he wasn't the standard *Duck Dynasty* incel. He still had that survivalist jawline, but it was cleaner. His shirt sleeves clung tightly to biceps that looked unfair. She hated herself for noticing. But she noticed.

"For the record," she said, "you're the worst man I've ever been zip-tied to."

"Same goes for you."

She smirked. "You get zip-tied to men a lot? In that case you're showing up with the wrong team."

The corner of his mouth twitched. "It's impressive you're still trying to recruit in handcuffs. Daddy Soros better pay overtime."

"I haven't called anyone 'daddy' in a while," Jennifer shot back. "Must hurt to hear."

His eyes flicked to her lips for a second—just a glitch. "Let me guess: four cats, one vibrator." He tilted his head toward her. "No boyfriend."

"And you must be one of those guys who eats steak three meals a day and takes cold showers because Jordan Peterson won't let you masturbate."

This time, he looked away. Like she'd struck something raw.

It felt nice to sting someone who deserved it. She stared ahead again, heart pounding in her ears. The warmth of his body still hovered beside hers.

Jennifer's friends stood in a clump nearby, not getting too close. Leah was alternating between gawking anxiously and checking her phone.

Her arms were falling asleep.

She checked him again. He was still looking away, face like a fortress.

The cops let them go twenty minutes later, no charges pressed.

They gave Jennifer back her phone and bag. She took them silently and wandered toward where her friends had been. They were gone now, so she hopped on a bus alone.

Her heart hadn't quite settled yet, and that guy's surprisingly tolerable smell still lingered in her nostrils.

It wasn't until the bus was moving that she noticed the screen on the cellphone they had handed her—a wallpaper photo of raw steak on an American flag plate.

She let out a slow breath. Where the fuck was her phone?

She slid the device into her hoodie pocket and leaned her forehead against the window.

***

Across town, Chet sat in his car and turned on the unfamiliar phone. The passcode screen was pastel. The background read: *Smash the state, drink water.*

He stared at it for a long moment. Then he leaned his head against the headrest and said, softly: "Fuck."

4

This Never Happened

Jennifer sat cross-legged on her floor, holding the chud's phone like it might bite. The screen was slightly greasy—she didn't want to guess why.

She'd already called herself from Marnie's number, twice, but no one had answered. Whoever he was, he hadn't figured out her passcode yet or was too principled to try. Most likely, too dumb.

She clicked around the home screen. The wallpaper was gone, replaced by a younger, cleaner him, no beard, standing shirtless in front of the Lincoln Memorial.

She made a soft, incredulous sound and opened Safari.

The first tab was a search for the phrase *is fluoride real*. The second: *top podcasts about freedom*. The third was halfway loaded: a private Twitter account called @BeefDaddy69. She clicked.

Pinned up top was a video of him shirtless in a park, talking about the benefits of cold plunges while doing kettlebell swings.

Jennifer lowered the phone and let out a sigh. Then she clicked to see what else he was into.

She found a playlist called "Ripped and Ready." A Notes app file titled *Things I'd fight for* (1. raw milk 2. Julian Assange 3. future wife).

She set the phone down but didn't move away.

***

Chet had spent the last hour in digital silence, staring at the phone.

He'd tried unlocking it with "1234" and "marx," then stopped, vaguely ashamed of himself.

Eventually, he realized he could still open Control Center. From there, he tried swiping into the camera. Surprisingly, it worked.

Her photos were mostly protest shots—blurred figures, signs, one haunting close-up of a boot print in what looked like spilled oat milk. Then selfies—tired, then glaring, then smoldering like they were meant for some soft-dicked loverboy. She was holding a beeswax candle in one like it was a weapon. He found that...confusing.

Her Notes app had a series of all-caps affirmations (*WHEN THEY GO LOW, WE SHUT IT DOWN*), then a link to a WikiHow article titled *Calling Men In*, then a recipe for something called Anti-Colonial Soup (carrot, turmeric, onion, ghee). He read the list of ingredients twice.

Then there was a poem:

Make Love, Then Dismantle the Police

Do not come in me like you come to conclusions.

Do not weaponize stillness.

I will kiss you and still throw the rock.

My body is not a detour from the revolution—

it is part of the route.

Chet sat with that as if deep in thought, then realized he wasn't.

He opened her Instagram. The bio said _Medic. Mouthy. Mostly kind._ There was a link to something called her Anti-Finsta. He clicked and watched a video of her smoking cloves while reading a _CrimethInc_ zine aloud. He found himself smiling. Something about her straight posture, or the seriousness in her voice as she read her terrorist brain rot like it was the Constitution.

Chet swiped. A reel played. It was her dancing to a remix of "Work Bitch" in a parking garage. She smiled once mid-dance, briefly, like she'd surprised herself.

His palms were sweating. "Shit," he muttered, then he opened Contacts.

***

The chud's phone buzzed, startling her. She didn't answer.

A minute later, a text popped up:

Are you the one with the anti-colonial soup recipe? I have your phone.

She stared at it a moment. Typed:

are you the guy who tagged your location "freedom zone" on instagram?

He replied:

That was mostly ironic.

She didn't believe him.

your notes app is 90% protein powder calculations.

A beat. Then:

Sorry if reading about protein triggered you.

She let out a laugh, then checked the room to confirm she was alone. She responded:

nice pics btw. did your nipples consent to being that patriotic?

He didn't reply for a while. When he did, it was:

Work Bitch dance was already taken :'(

Jesus. How much of her phone had he been through? She typed:

you're a creep. I'm putting the numbers for some therapists in your phone.

She saw the bubbles start, then stop, then start again.

I'd rather be waterboarded by Fauci than talk to you again. Meet me at the vape cafe on 11th. Noon. No molotov cocktails please.

Jennifer stared at the message, then closed the phone and pressed it to her chest.

***

Jennifer was sitting cross-legged on the bathroom counter, applying winged eyeliner, when Marnie wandered past and paused in the doorway.

"Where are you going?"

Jennifer didn't look at her. "Nowhere."

Marnie gave Jennifer a once over. "That's a lot of liner for nowhere."

Jennifer capped the eyeliner. She did look good. "I'm returning a phone."

"A date?"

"The farthest thing from it." She pulled on her tank top and checked herself once in the mirror. These weren't her most flattering jeans, but they weren't bad.

Marnie shrugged and made her way to the kitchen.

Jennifer started toward the door, then stopped. She pulled out the phone and opened it to one of the selfies. "Hey, Marnie?"

Marnie reappeared. "Yeah?"

"The person who has my phone is that QAnon asshole I got detained with at the protest." She held up the phone and Marnie reached for it. Jennifer didn't let go. "This is him. If I don't come back in an hour...maybe send a group?"

"Are you serious right now?"

"Unfortunately."

Marnie was studying Jennifer with an odd look on her face. "Jenn, shouldn't someone come with you?"

"No. It's fine, I just want to get this over with."

"If you don't come back, I'm going to call the cops."

"It'll be fine. I'm just returning a phone."

"But this guy is, like, actually dangerous."

Jennifer shook her head, pressed down the door handle, then bumped her hip against the door so it cracked open. "Everything is dangerous under late capitalism."

***

The vape cafe was called Exhalé and it sat on a quiet street corner between an expensive beauty salon and a tattoo parlor. Some mossy patio furniture was arranged out front alongside a chalkboard sign that said *Vape Your Truth*.

When Jennifer walked up, Chet was already posted up against the storefront with his arms crossed, looking uncomfortably out of place. Her eyes scanned the area for any threats. He was looking at her now and gave a brief, awkward wave, like a dad might.

She walked toward him, sizing him up in her mind. He was tall with a cocky posture. Broad shoulders, chest well-sculpted. Obviously strong, sure, but she knew enough self-defense to take him if she needed to.

She stopped just out of arm's reach and held up his phone. "Raw steak. Called it."

He rolled his eyes and produced hers. "Anti-Finsta? Really?"

A couple vaped on a nearby bench. One of them coughed too hard then looked around self-consciously.

Jennifer tilted her head. "So, this is your vibe? Freedom and emotional damage?"

"Better than writing love poems to the revolution."

She felt her cheeks heat and hoped the flush wasn't visible. "You have...so many protein powder recipes."

"Make Love, Then Dismantle the Police? How is it the Police Department's fault that your snowflake boyfriend can't get you off?"

Jesus Christ. He was thorough. She'd never shown her poetry to anyone before. "You read that?"

"Twice," he said.

"You liked it," she said, grinning.

"I couldn't believe how bad it was, so I had to check again."

Jennifer raised an eyebrow and looked him up and down. His jeans fit better than expected. "You're not as stupid as your Twitter," she said.

"Thanks. You're not as batshit as your Instagram."

Somehow during this exchange they'd ended up standing closer. It felt like she was leaning forward against her will. She glanced at her feet and then up at him. She could feel his breath against her. An unwelcome warmth spread through her belly.

"Okay," she said abruptly. "Let's do this." Jennifer held his phone out cautiously. He reached out and she felt a buzzing in her head. He was kind of sexy, in a disgusting way she would never admit to anyone. When he grasped the phone, she didn't let go. Her fingers tightened, nails grazing his knuckles. "Mine too." She extended her other hand expectantly.

He drew in a deliberate breath, eyes steady on hers, and raised her phone in reply. As she grasped it, he held on. Their fingers overlapped, stubborn and warm.

"On three," he said, openly flicking his eyes over her.

"One."

They counted together, matching each other's cadence.

"Two."

She was suddenly aware of her underwear clinging to her skin.

"Three."

They both let go, phones exchanged, stepping back in unison like they were ending a fencing match.

At that precise moment, a suited man on an electric scooter barreled past and clipped them both, sending them sprawling. Chet's knee buckled as he went down and Jennifer fell forward, landing on his chest. When their momentum stopped, they paused, breathing heavily.

He smelled familiar.

His eyes flicked to her lips and back to her eyes quickly. Then, he touched her face and she didn't stop him.

Her fingers found the edge of his shirt and curled there. His belly was warm against her knuckles.

They kissed—sudden, clumsy, hot. He tasted good. His stubble rubbed against her chin. Her pelvis pressed instinctively into him. Nearby, wind rustled a plastic bag caught on a bush.

She was kissing a fucking Nazi right now. A jolt of confusion ripped through her and she pulled back. "Wait, no."

Jennifer stood and checked her surroundings. The vaping couple had made their way inside.

He was standing now, too, eyes fixed on her, palms open.

A crow landed in the street and pecked at a tattered bag of potato chips.

Jennifer took a few steps back. Her face was hot. "What the fuck was that?"

He raised his eyebrows, mouth open like a dumbass. Then he laughed nervously and shook his head. "I don't know, I—I'm sorry. Heat of the moment." His expression softened into sincerity.

She wanted to punch him in the face but decided against it. "This never happened," she said.

"Yeah," he said, studying her with a puzzled expression like she was a media literacy exam. "Agreed."

"I mean it." She pointed at him. "If you tell anyone, I'll kick your fucking ass."

He made a dismissive face then nodded. "Mutually assured destruction. Trust me. I have a girlfriend."

Jennifer laughed incredulously. "I don't give a fuck about your sad tradwife girlfriend, dude. Just stay the fuck away from me."

He took a step back, holding his hands up like he thought she was losing her shit.

She wasn't losing her shit. This guy was a psycho.

"I'm sorry," he said. "Never happened, all good. Take care."

Jennifer shook her head, deciding whether to say more but there was nothing more to say. She turned and walked toward the bus stop, glancing over at herself in the reflection of the storefront windows to make sure he wasn't following her. He wasn't. She picked up her pace anyway.

Once she was around the corner, she stopped and looked back. No one was behind her.

She pulled out her phone and looked at the home screen for a second, then opened her camera and checked her face. Beads of sweat clung to her forehead and her lips were flushed.

She touched her mouth then stared at her fingers.

5

Other Lovers, Similar Positions

Chet Beefwell wasn't in love with Roxy Steel.

He didn't even particularly like her, not in the conventional way. But she had nearly half a million followers, a verified badge, and the kind of sharp, symmetrical face that made you think she'd never once doubted herself in a dressing room.

They met the previous summer at a tactical strength seminar. She was giving a demonstration on post-deadlift cortisol suppression; he was there to promote his new magnesium-infused beef jerky brand, Jerkin' for Liberty.

Roxy approached him while he was laying out samples. She picked up a pack and turned it over in her hands. "You raw batch or slow cure?"

Chet cocked his head. "Raw."

She nodded approvingly. "Bold."

By the end of the day, she'd tagged him in three posts, referred to him as "nutrient sovereign," and invited him back to her apartment to talk joint health. That night they dry-humped on a yoga mat in the glow of two ring lights while a Bluetooth speaker blared Tom MacDonald songs.

Now, a few months into their relationship, it seemed they were publicly a couple. He didn't ask and she didn't clarify.

To be honest, Chet wasn't even sure Roxy knew his last name. But she laughed at his jokes just enough to feel like they were in on something. Sometimes she'd take pictures of his hands while he was reading; she said it made her followers go feral. And he liked the way she would film sprints in the park, then caption the videos with Marcus Aurelius quotes.

They had sex like two people trying to win a bet they hadn't made aloud. She scratched his back so much it hurt, and he whispered praise into her ear that made her moan.

Still, when he woke up beside her in the middle of the night, he often felt like a crisis actor in a false flag that would never be staged.

One night, they sat on barstools at her kitchen counter sipping post-workout shakes. Her apartment smelled like tallow and peppermint oil. The lighting was cool and calculated, and the walls were plastered with sponsor banners: butcher boxes, liver pills, soy candles with names like Freedom Musk and Assault Pine.

Roxy absent-mindedly swiveled half-turns on her stool, taking long, slow sips and watching Chet closely. When she caught his eye, she put her blender bottle down and rested an elbow on the counter. "You know," she said, "you're the first man I've met in years who doesn't flinch when I mention bone marrow."

She had a way of looking at him at times like this, eyes big and glowing. Roxy's energy was like a steady freight train, barreling toward some future where she was wearing a red, white, and blue jumpsuit telling a stadium full of rabid right-wingers that the key to owning the libs was subscribing to her workout program.

Chet smiled faintly.

She kissed him efficiently with a closed mouth. Her lips tasted like chocolate and spearmint. "I'm serious," she continued. "We could be something. Like...the power couple that reminds America what testosterone looks like."

Chet was unsure what to say. Before he had to come up with a reply, she was leaning in, elbows on the counter, eyes sharp. "Chetty, I think you're about to blow up online."

Chet smirked. "We'll see."

"Those videos at the riots could really help," she said. She twirled a lock of bleach-blonde hair with her finger. "Though, they've been a little...*anemic* lately, haven't they?" She scanned his face. "Those thugs aren't looking as violent as they used to in your footage."

Chet glanced down. Her ass looked good on that stool. It always did. "They've been calmer."

"Well, you used to do more to wind them up. And that footage was really good."

He studied her but didn't say anything.

"The guys that get really big? They have a knack for getting clips of these people where they're really worked up and showing how depraved they are."

Chet shifted on the stool. That was true. A lot of streamers made a name for themselves by finding the worst of the worst of the left. Those were the kind of clips that had gotten him riled up in the beginning. "I want them to be less depraved," Chet countered.

Roxy made a face. "Sure. But people need to see the truth about those goons." She spun to face him and put a hand on his knee. "And sometimes the job of content creators is to help these people really show the camera who they are."

In the living room, a mounted TV played a silent loop of him and Roxy from her story archive. She'd added music—some orchestral remix of Toby Keith—and the caption: *American Love Isn't Dead, Just Deadlifting.*

"I'm just saying," Roxy continued. "There's a big wave we're riding. We should both just try and be the best content creators we can be. You and me, together? Forces of nature."

Chet stared into his shake. It looked like an unnamed galaxy.

***

Jennifer Soyvenus was still sleeping with Dev.

They weren't technically dating anymore, not since their "mutual uncoupling" via Google Docs six months ago. But Dev had a way of always being around that Jennifer usually tolerated, and sometimes even found comforting.

Dev and Jennifer had dated for a year after meeting at a mutual activist friend's party. Back then, Dev was the go-to guy to make flyers for protests and mutual aid events. It had taken Jennifer about six months to realize she never saw him turn up at one of those things unless there was booze and the women were dressed in something other than black bloc.

Marnie, for her part, had been against the Dev situation the whole time, and Jennifer usually felt aligned with her on matters of the heart. Early in their friendship, Jennifer and Marnie had bonded over having parents who inexplicably stayed in loveless and resentful marriages.

Privately, Jennifer felt the betrayal by her own mother was even more aggravating because, unlike Marnie's, she had the means to leave. But this was the type of thing she would never say to Marnie out of fear it would sound condescending.

Dev had recently launched a podcast called *Trauma but Make It Thirsty*. His latest episode was titled, "Reclaiming the Daddy Wound Through Ethical Exhibitionism."

Somehow always housed but never housed, Dev was currently camping out in his friend Lola's backyard, which he referred to as a lifestyle choice. Lola had enormous green eyes and a pixie cut and made her own jewelry out of stuff she found at flea markets.

One night when Dev was over, Jennifer checked the fridge for a kombucha she'd been saving. It was gone.

Dev was sitting on the floor, editing audio and eating seaweed crisps.

"Did you drink my kombucha?" she asked.

He looked up innocently. "There were kombuchas in the fridge," he said. "I assumed they were communal."

"There was one, and I was saving it."

A beat. "I didn't think this was the kind of house where we hoard carbonated beverages."

She stared at him. He stared back.

Later that night, he cried into her shoulder during a documentary about forest defense activists. She rubbed his back and stared at the oven clock intently.

A few days later, he texted, *Hey, random idea. Could I stay at yours for a while? Just until the podcast gets monetized. Spotify's being sketchy with numbers lately :/*

She didn't respond, but he showed up with a backpack and a yoga mat anyway.

That night after sex, Dev asked her if she had come. She rolled away and glared at the door to her bedroom, pulling the comforter tight. It was damp and scratchy all at once.

She felt Dev's fingers on her arm, tracing a line. He scooched in closer and his hip knocked against her ass. "You're pulling away," he whispered. "I feel it."

Jennifer sighed. She rolled back around and buried her face in his chest so she wouldn't have to look at him. "You're using me," she said.

Dev's scent was muted by familiarity. It always turned her on when it had been a while, then lost its allure the moment she'd come.

"I'm not using you," Dev said. "I love you."

Jennifer pulled the covers over her head. "You drank my kombucha and you're staying here for free and we broke up like a year ago."

She heard him sigh. "We don't have to stop knowing each other just because we aren't in some, like, hetero-monogamous box."

"Whatever, dude. Fuck."

He paused, then shifted up in bed. "Is there someone else?"

Jennifer let out a single, flat laugh. "You're projecting," she said, emerging from the covers again.

"No. I'm intuitive."

Jennifer rolled out of bed and stood, searching the floor half-heartedly for her underwear. The room was cold and she should pee and the bathroom would be cold, too. "You're exhausting," she said.

But didn't make him leave.

***

The next day, Dev was at the farmers market, probably performing emotional availability in front of some sauerkraut vendor.

Jennifer had told him she had cramps. She lay in bed, sun cutting thin lines across the sheets, her phone on Do Not Disturb. A half-read copy of *How to Do Nothing* perched face down on her nightstand.

It felt good to have the bed to herself. She had only a t-shirt on and the mattress cover material felt rough against her ass.

She pressed her legs together, then relaxed them as her fingers found her clit.

At first, she pictured something clean and aesthetic. A bathtub. Scented candles. A man grabbing her by the waist and pulling her in closer. His hands groping her breasts and thighs. His face—Chet's face?

She stopped and opened her eyes.

She couldn't. He was revolting. Physically, emotionally, ethically.

She bit down on the blanket and braced for a new story. She would think of a better man. A kind man. Penn Badgley.

It was Penn Badgley who was gently pressing his palm down on her stomach as she fanned out her legs. Penn Badgley—

She stopped again and lay there a few moments, finger idly circling her stomach.

As she tried again, her mind turned—unintentionally, but entirely—back to Chet and the way his hands had gripped her waist outside the vape cafe. The way his breath stuttered when she almost bit his lip.

She pressed her palm down harder and her hips curled instinctively. Her breath quickened, the blanket straining against her open mouth.

She hated this. Hated that her body didn't care about her morals. Hated that her arousal was a betrayal of everything she thought she stood for.

She let herself go deeper. Chet was tied to a chair, arms behind his back, thighs spread just enough to make him vulnerable. His shirt was ripped, chest exposed. Waiting.

She stood over him in the vision, tall and controlled, leather harness tight around her ribcage.

"You want this?" she asked, running a finger down his chest.

"Yes," he said. His voice was rough. Honest.

She slid her palm back and circled her clit with her fingers, spreading her wetness around herself.

"Read," she instructed, handing him a worn copy of *The Second Sex.*

He started, voice trembling. "Woman? Is—is not born—but becomes one…"

Jennifer squirmed and gripped the mattress. She felt her pulse throbbing in her clit. She pictured herself climbing into his lap, straddling him, pressing down without letting him in.

He was groaning. She was rocking slowly, controlling the pace. Controlling him.

She felt tingles build throughout her body.

Finally, she let him inside. They both trembled.

They came at the same time. Her forehead to his.

Back in reality, Jennifer's body arched and she came with a choked gasp. Her hands clenched the damp sheets.

Then everything was still. She felt light sweat on her forehead and her body relaxed. The blankets were cool as they clung to her skin.

She lay there a moment, hearing her heart pounding in her ears. Then she pulled the blanket over her face. "Fuck."

6

Takedowns

Two weeks after the vape cafe incident, Chet went to a co-ed self-defense class run by a nonprofit dedicated to "helping autonomous individuals take responsibility for their own safety."

Really, he was only there because Roxy had a brand deal with the studio and said they needed to "stay visible." She arrived in a monochrome fit—cropped track jacket, matte leggings, wraparound sunglasses—at dusk, leading him by the hand like a misbehaving child.

"I just need to get a few stories before warmups," Roxy said into her phone camera as they breezed past the front desk.

Chet squinted at the screen trying to work out whether she was talking to him or a stream, but it was hard to know.

Outside, Jennifer was crossing the parking lot with Marnie, Leah, Dev, and Mark.

It had taken months of prodding to get them all to agree to come to a training with her. She reminded them multiple times it was their responsibility to be able to defend themselves if things got violent at an action.

"Those gyms are always full of Nazis," Leah had protested.

"That means they're learning to fight but we aren't," Jennifer shot back.

As they approached the door, Jennifer reminded them to focus on the mission at hand. "It's not gonna be all leftists in there." She was wearing black leggings and a vintage Riot Grrrl tank top that belonged to Marnie. "But we need to learn to fight if they're going to."

Dev took a meaningful sip of his Gatorade. "If anyone needs a safe man in that space at any time during this class, call my name." He adjusted his beanie. "Remember—we protect us."

The air in the studio smelled like old rubber mats and eucalyptus sanitizer, and the fluorescent lights flickered with just enough irregularity to feel like a warning.

Jennifer scanned the room—these things always drew an odd collision of lefty activists, right-wing coded fitness freaks, and hard-to-clock optics-chasers. Turnout was decent and scattered murmurs echoed off the walls.

"Some of these people are definitely chuds," Leah said under her breath.

Marnie nodded.

"It's an MMA studio," Jennifer said. "I've been here a few times. Just keep your head down and get the info you need."

Leah's eyes flicked around nervously. She glanced at Jennifer, then turned back to Marnie. "The smell is...memorable."

Someone's shoe screeched on the mat.

Jennifer stepped up to the front desk, still surveying the scene.

There he was. In mesh shorts and a shirt that said "Get Ripped, Stay Vigilant." He was standing behind a bleach-blonde woman with some of the angriest biceps Jennifer had ever seen, already looking back at her with a stoic expression.

He gave a single downward nod.

Shit. She looked away and grabbed a waiver from the stack at the desk, then checked again.

He was still watching her.

The bleach-blonde woman was talking to a bald man holding a clipboard. She pushed him playfully, then reached back and grabbed Chet's arm as the man stepped to the center of the room and blew a whistle.

Jennifer felt a hand on her back and flinched. It was Dev. He gave her a hurt look, and she took a step closer, leaning her hip into him.

Throughout warmups, Jennifer kept glancing across the room. Chet was doing everything with perfect form, and she hated him for it. He seemed to avoid looking anywhere near her. She didn't know what to do with that, but the air between them felt thick and itchy.

"All right, everybody circle up," the instructor said. "Let's pair off and make some new friends. I'll count us off."

They wandered to the middle of the room as he began counting. He pointed at Chet and said, "One," then kept counting down the line.

Jennifer did a quick count. To her dismay, she was about to be paired with him. She tried to reposition herself between Leah and Marnie, but Leah gave an odd look and stood her ground.

Marnie glanced nervously between Leah and Jennifer.

"One," the instructor said, pointing at Jennifer, then he continued down the line.

Chet smiled but quickly regained composure.

The instructor clapped his hands. "Let's do this."

People found their partners and moved to open spaces on the mat.

Marnie lingered by Jennifer a moment, studying her. "You good?"

"I was just gonna make a joke," Jennifer said, waving her off. "I'll tell you later."

Marnie nodded and went to find her partner.

Chet appeared. "Hello," he said cautiously.

The instructor had returned to the front of the room. "We're doing controls and takedowns. If you've done these before, raise your hand."

Jennifer and Chet both put a hand up and then looked at each other.

Chet raised his eyebrows.

"Great," the instructor said. "Get started with some controls if you've done them. If you haven't, circle up for a quick demo."

Jennifer faced Chet expectantly.

He gestured to her. "After you."

Jennifer shook her head. "You start."

He pursed his lips. "Okay." Then he got in his stance and extended a hand toward her.

"You're supposed to grab me," Jennifer said. She took his hand and placed it on her shoulder. His palms felt firm and familiar in ways they shouldn't be. Her stomach tensed.

He nodded.

She shot her right arm up and grabbed his wrist. He tried to hold on as she found his elbow with her other hand and pressed, throwing her body weight into the motion so the pressure was just right.

He writhed a bit but eventually she had him bent over.

He tapped his hips and she released.

"Pretty good," he said, smirking.

"Fuck off," she said, squaring off with him again.

"Go for it," he said.

She stepped into him and grabbed the front of his shirt. There it was again—his scent. His breath was hot on her neck.

He grabbed her wrist firmly but cautiously. He began to gently lead her arm. She didn't move.

"You can actually try here," she said. "I won't break."

He sighed and pressed harder.

She strained, still able to resist. "Harder," she said.

They made eye contact and her skin tingled.

"You let me know if I'm hurting you," he said.

"Just do it," she said.

He moved, swift and forceful, and pain shot through her arm as he twisted it behind her. Her ass brushed against his hip and he let go.

She laughed and straightened out. "Okay. Now takedowns." She turned away from him and craned her neck to catch his eye. "Grab me like you mean it this time."

Chet stepped into her, and she felt the full, solid force of his body against hers. He wrapped his arms around her and a gooey warmth spread through her stomach.

Jennifer reminded herself who this guy was. A guy who stood shoulder-to-shoulder with assholes waving Blue Lives Matter flags. A guy who captioned his pics with "freedom zone." A guy who, right now, was breathing in her ear like he'd just surfaced from a dream where his head was buried between her legs.

She jammed a foot back and pressed her right knee against his. Then she pried her fingers under his palms, lunged forward, and strained to twist her body enough to flip him.

He hit the mat with a thud.

"Are you okay?" she asked. She went to help him up, but he dismissed her hand with a wave.

"Totally fine," he said. "Don't get your feelings hurt. You did good."

Jennifer rolled her eyes and stepped toward him again. "Turn around," she said. He smirked and turned his back to her and she looked down, observing how tight his butt was, then just as quickly hated herself for noticing.

She pressed herself against his back and wrapped her arms around his chest, bracing herself for him to pick her up and fling her.

The instructor blew his whistle. "Let's wrap it up!"

Chet straightened gently then stepped away.

"The fuck?" she said.

He turned back to her and shrugged. "You heard him," he said. "Guess I won't be throwing you around today."

***

After class, Jennifer regrouped with her friends near a bulletin board at the back of the room. Leah was complaining about the instructor's "aggressive energy" and Dev was explaining how the padded mats were off-gassing microplastics. Marnie listened solemnly like this was news.

Across the room, Roxy had Chet pinned in place, angling her phone just right as he wiped sweat off his brow. She whispered something and handed him a shaker bottle. He took it like a prop.

"We're here at BaseLine Defense," Roxy said, filming over her shoulder, "just getting that functional burn. Right, babe?"

Chet flashed a tight-lipped smile. "Hey, you know us, always up for a work-out." He was looking past the phone and across the room at Jennifer.

She was standing in the back with her snowflake militia, facing away from him. Her leggings were just the right amount of tight. It was the first time he'd gotten a chance to really notice her ass.

She shifted on her feet. Clocked him looking at her.

Fuck.

She looked at the hallway, then back at Chet, then peeled off from her group like she was either going to refill her water bottle or throw up.

Roxy was reviewing her clips.

He rubbed the back of his neck. "I'm gonna take a leak," he muttered. "Meet you outside." He didn't wait for her response.

The hallway was quiet, cold, lit like a school at night. Chet reached the bathroom first and opened the door without hesitating. It clicked shut behind him and he walked over to the sink.

A second later, it opened again.

Jennifer lingered by the door, arms folded. Her skin was warm with a post-sparring flush and strands of hair clung to her cheeks.

The fluorescents buzzing overhead cast Chet in a blunt, angular light: thick arms, sweat line down his sternum, shirt stretched tight across his chest. He looked big and solid and he was breathing just a little too fast.

Jennifer cocked her head. "Not so afraid of gender-neutral bathrooms anymore, are we?"

Chet smirked, eyes flicking over her. "The nice thing about a men's room is it's less chatty."

Jennifer raised an eyebrow. "Are you here to chat?" She took a few steps toward him then stopped.

He scratched the back of his head, biceps flexing with the movement, and stepped closer. "I'm here for all the normal reasons. Why did you follow me in?"

Jennifer looked at the outline of his thigh muscle under those loose mesh shorts. She hated how curious she was about how it would feel between her legs. She took a few steps closer. "I was headed here first, and you know it."

"I can leave if you want me to. But I don't think you do."

Jennifer paused. The strangeness of the moment tightened her stomach. She could scream for help. Tell him to fuck off. She could punch him in his smug face.

His eyes were searching hers. They were pretty, which was unfair.

She leaned in. "You have no idea what I want."

He lingered there, unflinching, his face inches from hers. "Okay. Then show me."

There was no way she was about to do this with him. The thought of it made her...uncomfortably close to wet.

She wobbled for a moment, unsure where she was about to end up, then took a step back. Chet relaxed his stance but didn't move.

Her friends would be waiting for her.

Chet watched her with wide eyes. The hint of an erection was beginning to poke its way through his shorts.

Jennifer stepped forward and pushed him once. He made an amused face and steadied himself.

Then she lunged and kissed him hard. Teeth. Tongue.

He kissed back. His mouth was urgent and possessive. A noise from somewhere low in his chest sent heat straight between her legs.

She stepped past him, mouth still locked to his, and backed into the sink, pulling him along. The cold ceramic rammed into the back of her thighs. He pressed himself into her and she moaned.

"This doesn't mean anything," she said breathlessly.

"Cool," he said, kissing down her jaw. "I won't put it in my diary later."

Her leggings were damp now, almost slick. "I still think you're a neo-Nazi."

"And I think if you weren't here with me, you'd be out firebombing some car dealership." His hand slid up her thigh, pausing just beneath the curve of her ass, not quite touching where she needed.

Her breath hitched.

The mirror behind them was slightly fogged. The flickering light overhead turned everything surreal—pornographic and intimate at once.

"You're disgusting," she whispered.

"I've been working out," he whispered back. Then he nudged his thigh between her legs.

She grabbed the collar of his shirt, shoved him away, pulled him back in again, and ground her hips into his leg. She did it again and a shudder ripped through her.

Jennifer's breath came faster now. She hooked one leg around his, tilted her hips, and began moving against him.

He slid his hands over her ass this time and held tight.

"Fuck," she gasped, grinding harder. She palmed his face and pushed his head back. "Don't say anything."

"I wasn't going to," he said, squirming away from her hand.

She smacked him on the side of the head and he cursed under his breath.

He lifted her and carried her over to a nearby wall. Her back thudded against it as he slid his thigh between her legs again. His shorts were thin enough to feel how hard he was. Her pelvis moved on its own now. She pressed her mouth to his ear. "I would never, ever let someone like you inside me."

"I would never fall for your Marxist honeypot trap anyway," he replied, and placed his hand over her mouth and kissed her neck. She bit his palm as she moved faster, bunching his shirt in her fists.

He felt good. A wave of pleasure carried her forward, lost in the moment.

She came quietly on his leg, shaking, and let out one soft, broken moan into his hand.

For a long moment, neither moved.

His head rested on her collarbone. Then he stepped back, guiding her to the ground.

She tugged her tank top down and ran a hand through her hair.

Both remained silent, avoiding eye contact as they collected themselves.

Chet ran the tap, splashing cold water on his face.

She checked her reflection in the mirror. Smudged eyeliner. Red cheeks. She left it.

Chet looked her in the eyes through the mirror. Without saying anything, he opened the door and exited the bathroom.

Jennifer hovered over the sink, catching her breath. She wiped her forehead with the back of her hand and walked back out.

Folks had mostly left the studio. The instructor said something to her and she thanked him for the class and gathered her things. She could hear her pulse in her ears.

She headed for the exit and checked her phone. A text from Marnie from five minutes ago: *outside.* She stepped out the doors and saw them gathered across the lot, but she kept her eyes on the screen. She had two missed calls from Dev, followed by a message three minutes ago: *where are you?*

7

Housecall

It was 11:48 p.m. Chet lay in bed, staring at the ceiling. Shirtless, restless.

The house was quiet except for the hum of a fridge he no longer trusted after an alarming Reddit binge a few weeks ago.

He adjusted his shorts. His dick had been hard ever since he left the gym, and he hated it.

Roxy had asked if he wanted to stay over, but he told her he needed to edit some audio. Now he was kicking himself for not taking the opportunity to let off some of this steam.

He was equal parts horny and confused after the day's events. He'd never really pictured what a terrorist's orgasm might look like before, but now he couldn't get the sound of Jennifer's moans out of his mind. Or the way her mouth felt pressed against his hand.

He tried to think of anything else—football before Taylor Swift cucked the NFL, kettlebell routines, the time a cop patted him on the back and said, "Stay sharp, brother"—but it kept coming back to her. Her ass in those yoga pants. Her delusional hatred of Americans. That stupid soup recipe.

He wasn't going to masturbate. Jax had been saying it for a while, and he was beginning to realize why it might be true: spilling your life force anywhere other than into a tradwife's pussy or mouth—or maybe on her tits depending on who you asked—was a globalist impulse. One that eroded your strength from the inside.

There was no way he was actually into some woke mob zombie whose idea of a good time was vandalizing small businesses. He needed a cold shower.

Instead, he went online and started watching 8K deepfakes of liberal cities burning—Portland, Chicago, Austin. Screaming masked vegans with armpit hair setting things on fire.

He wondered if she shaved her armpits. Or her legs even.

He wondered how she looked naked.

He could picture it pretty well, actually.

Fuck.

Chet sat up and punched his dick. Hard. Twice. Three times. Just to show it who was boss.

Now he was somehow even harder. He dropped to the floor and began doing pushups over his dumbbell so that his dick touched it on the way down. Discipline. Control. Strength.

His brain wouldn't stop. He imagined Jennifer inviting him over, naked except for a skimpy Karl Marx crop top. She stationed him on a couch, and he watched as she mounted some Adam Friedland-looking soy boy and rode him.

Then she turned to Chet and crawled toward him on the ground. He imagined her mouth, the suction, her eyes locked with his as she drained him then spat his semen into a glitter envelope addressed to Planned Parenthood.

Instead of coming, he collapsed on the floor, chest heaving, shame churning his stomach. He lay there for several minutes, then crawled into bed, eyes wide open in the dark.

11:55 p.m.

He turned his phone over in his hand. No new texts.

He scrolled through their messages. He selected the entire thread, hovered over the Delete All button, then stopped.

He closed Messenger and put his phone face down on his chest.

She seemed to really know her stuff on a mat.

"I'd never let someone like you inside of me," she had said. Then she came on his leg.

Chet wandered over to his hamper and picked up his gym shorts, studying them. Brought them to his nose for a whiff.

Something inside him buzzed.

He walked back to his bed and picked up his phone.

He typed, *You up?* and hit send.

Then he waited.

***

"Are you...listening?" The question came from Marnie.

Jennifer had been looking at herself reflected in her wine and wondering if there was something different about her face or if it was just distorted by the glass. She looked at Marnie, who was now sitting up on the couch, concerned. "I didn't catch that last bit, sorry. What were you saying?"

Marnie gave a quizzical look and lay back down. "Yoga. Doesn't matter."

"Sorry, babe. I'm spacey today."

"Daydreaming about that chud from the MMA studio?"

Jennifer's heart gave one declarative thud. "What?"

Marnie sat up again, smiling. "I'm just kidding. That guy was something else though, wasn't he?"

Jennifer wondered what her own face looked like. Her cheek muscles felt stiff like dry cement. "Which one? There were a few chuds there—"

"You know, the one you got paired with at the end? He showed up with Muscle Milk Barbie."

"Oh, him," Jennifer said nonchalantly. "I was thinking more about why Leah was being such an ice-queen."

"Was he respectful or, like, a creepo?"

"He was a dude at an MMA studio. I don't know."

Marnie absently fiddled with the drawstring of her hoodie. "Leah was just...being Leah." A beat. "Anyway, I think you intimidate her."

"She was like that at the protest, too. I told you about that, right?"

"Yeah, you did, Jenn."

"They ditched me," Jennifer said. "They were holding signs that said *This is what solidarity looks like*, but then I got arrested, and they just, like, peeled off for brunch or something."

"I thought you were just detained."

An uncomfortable silence settled between them.

Jennifer raised her shoulders in an unnaturally slow shrug.

Marnie raised her eyebrows. "Maybe they figured you were good without them. You're good in those situations. You get...tunnel-y."

"I wasn't being tunnel-y."

Marnie paused. "No, I didn't say you were. Just that sometimes, when you're in organizer mode, it's...hard to keep up."

Jennifer looked down, weighing her options, then muttered, "Well, at least I showed up."

Marnie gave a long, quiet blink and studied Jennifer's face as if deciding whether this was a fight. Finally, she said, "Well, I'm sorry they ditched you. I wouldn't have."

Jennifer drained her glass. "Thanks."

They sat in silence a moment, bathed in fluorescent light. Outside, a car rolled by on the wet street. Then Jennifer stood. "I'm headed to bed." She shuffled into her room without another word, shut the door, and started undressing.

Her phone buzzed. She picked it up.

You up?

It was Chet.

What the fuck?

Her mind was playing tricks on her. She looked again.

Not Dev. Chet, definitely Chet.

Her pulse quickened. She took off her shorts and absentmindedly flung them toward the hamper.

Was he joking? Or drunk?

The cold air made goosebumps on her legs.

The bathroom had been...good, but wrong.

She ran her hands over her thighs, thinking. She should ignore the text. Block him, even.

His hands though. His smell. His hard-on.

She stared at the screen. She could say *i am* and that would be a simple statement of fact.

She shouldn't text back.

She typed: *are you lost?* and hit send.

She set her phone on the dresser, then wandered over to the bed and stood there looking at it.

The phone buzzed behind her again.

She shouldn't check it.

She went back to the dresser.

Maybe I'm craving some post-colonial soup.

She rolled her eyes.

He was typing again.

Have to admit you impressed me on the mat today. And in the bathroom.

She thought, then texted: *wish i could say the same for you :/*

He started typing immediately, then stopped. Started. Stopped again. Then: *Not satisfied? I should make that up to you...*

This fucking Nazi was actually trying to booty call her right now.

She couldn't do that. She should stay here in her room, hiding from her full-of-shit roommate and even-more-full-of-shit ex-boyfriend and lie alone gloomily in bed pretending she hadn't absolutely loved grinding on this chud's thigh.

She typed: *maybe you should* and hit send, feeling immediately horrified with herself.

His reply came: *Should I come to you or...*

Absolutely not.

dude, there is no way i am telling you where i live

He didn't miss a beat:

Suit yourself.

Then he dropped a pin.

***

Jennifer hovered in his doorway, arms crossed, hoodie zipped up despite the warm temperature of the room.

Chet had let her in without a word—he didn't know what to say. Honestly, he couldn't believe she was really here.

"Do you want a drink?" he asked, shuffling toward the kitchen.

"No."

Her hands were tucked into her sleeves, and her eyes scanned him with a mix of desire and distrust.

"Not even water?"

The room was dim, lit only by the flicker of a combat-sports recap he'd left on mute.

Jennifer moved cautiously across the living room, studying the walls like she was looking for any reason to leave. "You didn't invite me over to give me a glass of water," she said, studying the American flag hanging over his couch. Then she nudged a dumbbell he'd left on the floor with her foot.

Even her profile was pretty. He couldn't believe he'd gotten this far with someone like her. "You know why I invited you." He let that hang in the air, waiting for her to look at him. When she did, he said, "What I don't get is why you came. Middle of the night. Knowing why."

"Jesus." She moved across the edge of the room, arcing toward him indirectly like a cat. Then she stopped just short of him. "Maybe I'm here to kill you."

Her proximity made his heart pound. She smelled sweet. Freckles speckled her nose, and her lips were flushed. He made his best attempt at a cocky smirk. "You're taking your sweet time."

"Is this your kink? Fucking Antifascists?"

He shook his head.

"I always assumed chuds like you were the worst lay imaginable."

"Is that your kink? Bad sex?"

She broke eye contact. "This place has premature ejaculation written all over it."

He took one step forward, resisting the urge to keep going. "Here you are," he said.

"Here I am." She was looking at him now like a challenge. His breath was shallow. The thrill of having her flirt back sent blood rushing to his crotch. It was now or never.

He moved in toward her. She stepped back until her thighs hit the edge of the couch. She put her hand up and he stepped forward until her fingertips touched his chest.

"I'm not doing this because I like you," she said.

"I'm not asking you to."

"You're not even the worst mistake I've made."

"You can leave if you really feel that way."

She glared. "Don't dare me."

He looked her in the eyes, then at her lips, then her eyes again and tilted his head.

"I still think you're dangerous," she said. "Ideologically. Spiritually. Possibly sexually."

"I'm not a fascist," he said. "Or whatever you think of guys like me."

"You follow Jordan Peterson and tagged your leg day workout 'biological essentialism.'"

He leaned in. "I don't even know what that means."

"Exactly."

He kissed her and she kissed back—surgical, searching, like she was trying to diagnose something. Her smell and taste filled every corner of his mind and he felt his erection straining against itself.

She yanked at his shirt. He lifted his arms like he was being frisked.

"Good boy," she muttered.

That did something to him. He scooped her up and set her down on the couch, kneeling between her legs.

"You like that?" she taunted as he kissed down her chest. "A little assertiveness from the deep state?"

"Oh, is it deep?"

She gripped his hair, pulled him in.

Their mouths crashed—messy, breathless.

His hand slid inside her leggings, then he paused.

"You can touch me," she said. "I'm still gonna believe in collective liberation tomorrow."

He licked his fingers then pushed inside, thumb circling her clit. "You're so wet for me," he breathed.

"You say that like you've earned it."

He tugged her leggings to her knees, kissed the inside of her thigh, and dropped his head between her legs. He heard her gasp, then felt her hand tugging his hair.

She tasted sweet. He ran a hand slowly over her thigh and gently sucked her clit into his mouth, tongue flicking.

A violent shudder moved through her body, and she clamped her legs around his head, let out an unmistakable yelp, then relaxed.

Holy shit.

He lifted his gaze to hers, heart hammering.

She caught her breath and grinned at him with a nod. Then, she removed her leggings entirely. "Bathroom," she instructed. "Now."

There, she stripped her hoodie over her head, bent over the sink, and looked at him through the mirror. "You're disgusting, and I hate everything you stand for."

He stepped into her and pressed against her entrance, his voice low. "You want me to fuck the patriotism back into you, don't you?"

She stared at him in the mirror, mouth parted. Then she reached back and guided him in.

She was wet, warm, incredible—he would need to pace himself. He started slow, then moved faster as she met him thrust for thrust.

"I feel like I'm about to get cancelled," she moaned.

He hooked his finger in her mouth and pulled her head back into him. "You're a bad, bad little commie, and I'm gonna fuck you until you come."

She closed her lips around his finger and sucked it deeper into her mouth, her teeth grazing his knuckles.

He thrust deeper. Skin against skin. Ragged breath. She looked like she might collapse in on herself like a society with no values.

She pressed a hand forcefully against the counter and pushed him back. He took himself out of her and she spun around to face him. Her nipples were flushed, and she tilted her chin up.

Chet stood still for a moment, breathing heavily. Her eyes were locked on his. He moved forward again and she lifted herself onto the counter and wrapped her legs around his waist. He grazed his mouth over her chest and she pulled his hair so hard it hurt.

He was inside her again and let out a groan. The bottom of his shaft slid against the edge of the counter with each thrust, tilting him higher into her.

She moaned.

He crashed his mouth into hers.

She kissed him and cooed, "Just like that."

He grabbed the back of her neck.

She looked at him with defiance, then tilted her head back and spat in his face. "Fucking Nazi," she said.

Holy shit did he like that. He slammed his palm against the mirror and thrust harder.

They came together and he let out a low grunt, forehead pressed into hers. Her body trembled, chest rising and falling rapidly against his.

He put his mouth against her neck and ran his hands over her back and hips. Her skin was soft and flushed. "I know it's late," he heard himself saying. "You can crash here if you want."

8

Different Strokes

Jennifer woke just before sunrise to a tentative blue-gray light in the room.

Soft snoring sounded beside her. Chet was still asleep, diagonal across the bed with one arm resting across his chest. His phone buzzed. He didn't stir.

She watched him for a moment. Slowly, she eased out of bed, eyes adjusting to the dim light.

Her clothes were scattered across the apartment. Hoodie in the bathroom. Leggings crumpled by the couch. She gathered them, dressing as she went, then slipped out the door.

Outside, the streetlights were flickering off. The only sounds were birds chirping and the groans of a nearby garbage truck. Her lip was swollen and there was a faint ache in her thighs.

She'd liked it—that was the part she couldn't shake. Snuck out in the middle of the night to see him, even.

She pulled her hood up and kept walking.

The front door of her house creaked when she came in. She moved down the hallway quietly, hoping to reach her room before—

"Hey." Marnie's voice came from the kitchen.

Jennifer froze.

Turning the corner, she found Marnie already at the table in her robe, sipping coffee. A single AirPod rested in the middle of the counter.

Jennifer offered a weak smile. "Hey." She paused a moment, pondering the most natural thing to say. "You're up early."

"So are you."

Jennifer chuckled. "I guess so."

"What's up?"

Jennifer floated to the kitchen table, placing a hand tentatively on the back of chair. "Didn't sleep well."

Marnie fell into an evaluative silence, then her eyes flicked to her phone and back to Jennifer. "You hear about the ICE facility?"

Jennifer shifted her weight. "What happened?"

"Big raid last night," Marnie said. "They detained like twenty people. There was a protest. Some chuds showed up, too."

"Jesus." Jennifer hadn't heard any of this. She'd been too busy fucking some red-pill bro to show up when it counted.

"There's gonna be another protest there tonight. Leah's going. And Mark."

"I should go, too," said Jennifer, walking to the cupboard. No clean mugs. "I'll text them. Are you coming?"

"I thought you might have been there last night. I was watching it on the stream and came to get you, but you were gone."

She should have been there. "Oh yeah, no."

Marnie tilted her head quizzically. "Where were you then? I thought you went to bed."

Without looking back, Jennifer replied, "I couldn't sleep and went out."

"With who?"

Jennifer shrugged. "Dev." She found a mug in the sink and grabbed a sponge.

"Hmm."

Jennifer ran the tap and started scrubbing.

Marnie said, "I didn't like how things left off last night."

She'd almost forgotten. She sighed and turned to face Marnie. "Yeah, me neither."

"Are you mad that I'm friends with Leah?"

Jennifer squeezed the sponge and watched a little stream of soap fall into the sink. "I don't really care about Leah one way or another."

It was true. Leah was an unserious person. Full of tweet-worthy one-liners but hardly important when push came to shove.

Marnie pursed her lips. "Are you gonna keep rubbing it in my face that I didn't go to one protest?"

In as gentle a tone as she could muster, Jennifer said, "It's been more than one."

"I missed a few," said Marnie.

"You stopped going," said Jennifer.

Marnie shifted. "Those things are getting crazy."

"I know. I'm the one who got attacked."

"So I can't be careful?"

Jennifer dug her thumbnail into the skin of her pointer finger until it hurt. "You can do whatever you want."

For a while, the only sound was the tap running. Then Marnie said, "You know, people would go easier on you if you went easier on them."

She shut off the tap. "Okay, so people don't like me?"

Marnie sighed. "People like you but you're..."

Jennifer waited for the rest to come, but the silence lasted too long. She looked back at Marnie, who was sitting at the table studying her. They made eye contact, both silent.

"Who were you with last night?" said Marnie.

"What?"

"Dev posted a TikTok at like midnight about radical alone time."

Fuck. It had been sloppy to say that. "Okay?"

"Is there something you aren't telling me?"

Jennifer shrugged. "Random hookup."

Marnie looked hurt. "So why did you say Dev?"

Jennifer wandered to the table and sat down. "I don't know. It was just a booty call with some rando. It felt silly."

Marnie gazed down at the table, fiddling with her mug. "We usually debrief that sort of thing."

There was a light pain in Jennifer's chest. "Yeah."

"Are we good?" Marnie looked up at Jennifer.

Careful to maintain eye contact, Jennifer took a deep breath. "Are we?"

"I wanna be."

"Me too."

The silence rested between them.

Marnie nodded in contemplation. Then she cleared her throat and said, "Maybe I'll go tonight."

"Okay," Jennifer said. This didn't feel like a win. "Your choice."

Marnie pursed her lips, then she put her AirPods away and stood. "Sure."

***

Chet guided the barbell back to the rack, then straightened.

Tyler stood behind him, wearing a camo-patterned weight vest. "Tonight, we need more of our guys out there. Their numbers keep growing, and I don't know what they're planning, but it is not going to be pretty."

Chet stood and took a drink of water. "I'll be there."

Tyler took his turn on the bench. "I told Jax to show up, too, but not to act too crazy. That dude would love to start a street brawl anytime, anywhere. I don't think it's the smartest way to operate, but I respect the balls."

Chet watched Tyler grip the bar. "Well, if he's serious about getting a job in law enforcement, he should be careful not to get into any compromising positions."

Tyler scoffed. "You really think that? I think ICE likes guys who are willing to lean in. I think he's auditioning."

Tyler was probably right about that. "Roxy asked me why we don't start shit anymore. Seems like she's on the same page as Jax."

"What did you say?"

"I said it looks better when they start it, but they just haven't been as crazy recently."

Tyler chuckled. "You getting soft on the libs, Beefwell?"

The gym was slow—neon lights humming, most of the machines sat empty. There was something surreal about the whole scene.

"Never."

Tyler made a face as he struggled to complete his rep. "You think you're gonna marry that woman?"

The question caught Chet off guard. "Why?"

"I don't know. She posts you all the time now. You two would be something. And you know she's a—uh, respectfully—she's a beautiful lady."

"I like keeping my options open," Chet said.

"Damn. Romantic."

Chet paused, trying to figure out how to say something that felt unsayable. He didn't really want to tell Tyler about Jennifer—didn't even want to think about her, not here—but he did want to know what he might think in theory. "I danced with this chick at a bar a few months ago. Smokeshow."

"You? Dancing? She must've been hot."

"Shoulda seen her. Dick-suckin' eyes, you know? That look where you just...know."

"And?"

"She said she was a Democrat."

Tyler made a choking sound as he sat up on the bench. "What'd you do, douse yourself in sanitizer and run?"

Chet felt something tightening in his stomach. "I wasn't that dramatic about it. But yeah, I made my exit. Thing is, I got home and regretted it a little. I mean, if it's just tail, is it that bad?"

"If she's hot, sure. But never date one. You want a feminazi hit-and-quit? Go for it. Different strokes."

"Okay. So, Democrat chick, hit and quit only. But what about...a full-blown commie?"

Tyler stood and wiped his forehead with a towel. "I don't even know how that would happen." He stepped up to Chet, a hair too close. "You think the Americans were sucking off the Brits before the Boston Tea Party?"

Chet shrugged.

Tyler laughed, slapping him on the back. "Communism's like syphilis, my friend. You catch it through your dick and then it eats your brain."

Chet stared at the rubber tiles, silent for a moment. Then he positioned himself on the bench and gripped the bar.

9

Mid-Stream

Leah arrived just as Jennifer was finishing dinner.

Marnie had spent most of the day in her room, and Jennifer had taken a nap then lazed around the house, checking her phone frequently. She saw no reason to send the typical next-day text to Chet. The whole thing had obviously been a fluke. He hadn't sent one either, and she wondered if that was just how he was or if he was also hoping they could forget the whole thing and move on.

Leah and Jennifer made awkward small talk, both uncertain whether Marnie was actually going to come. Neither wanted to be the one to ask. Jennifer had only spoken with Leah one-on-one a handful of times, and they mostly talked about Leah's third-grade class. Leah was clashing with the administration over book ban policies put forth by the school board. She had a blunt but sincere way of speaking, which Jennifer found charming despite herself. With no one else around, their dynamic felt notably less confrontational.

Marnie emerged from her room with a sense of ceremony and nervous energy—black-clad, carrying a small shoulder bag. "Taking the Six?"

"Six to the Fifteen," Jennifer replied. "Do you need a face covering?"

Marnie returned a close-lipped smile and shook her head gently. "Got one."

"I have some N95s, too," Leah chimed in.

"Thank you," Jennifer said, immediately feeling over-formal. "Let's do it."

The bus smelled like body odor and Taco Bell. The trio found seats toward the back and began scrolling Twitter for updates.

Leah pulled up a left-wing streamer. A solid group was already there, and the cops had just finished their first round of teargassing.

"There's a lot of counter-protesters there tonight," Leah said, scanning Jennifer and Marnie's faces as she spoke.

Jennifer pulled up a right-winger's stream. Her phone blared and she quickly turned her volume to zero. "And a lot of unfriendly streamers."

"They're such assholes," Marnie muttered.

"You watch those guys?" Leah asked.

"It's helpful to see how they're covering it," Jennifer said. "You know, they tend to get more views than left-wingers."

"Really?" Leah raised her brows. "There's so many more of us."

Jennifer shrugged. "Our videos get watched by local leftists. Theirs get watched by right-wingers across the country."

The bus stopped and a wave of people boarded. Some folks looked like they were headed to the protest as well, but no one Jennifer recognized.

An older woman was making her way through the aisle, scanning for an open seat.

"Here you are," said Leah, standing.

The woman waved her off. "I'm okay."

"Take it," Leah said. "Really. I feel like standing anyway."

***

It was dark when they got to the ICE facility. A large crowd of about forty was gathered, hazy in the floodlights. Tear gas lingered in the air.

Activists held handmade signs: *Stop Tearing Families Apart* and *ICE = Modern Day Gestapo*. A mutual aid group had set up a canopy tent over a table stacked with flyers and water bottles. A Bluetooth speaker blared dubstep.

Mark stood off to the side of a few larger clumps of people in the street. He waved and dipped his mask down so they would recognize him.

Leah and Marnie masked up almost immediately upon getting off the bus, but Jennifer was just now pulling up her hoodie and wrapping a black scarf around her mouth.

The facility's gates were closed. Two agents in full combat gear stood at ground level, but several others were positioned on the roof.

Jennifer spotted the glint of something and saw a shadowy figure up top. Sniper.

Counter-protesters lurked across the street, waving American flags and shouting insults. Right-wing streamers occasionally weaved through the crowd, shoving lavalier mics in people's faces and speaking with exaggerated calm until their targets shooed them away. The process would repeat a few times until a fight broke out, then other protesters intervened to walk the streamers back across the street.

"We should break their fucking phones," Leah said. "They're just here to doxx us."

"It's risky being here," Jennifer said. "We have to accept that. If we break their phones, that's a crime and it looks bad."

"To who?"

"To everyone who's on our side but is scared to join us," Jennifer replied.

"If they care more about some Nazi's phone than they do about stopping the deportations, they aren't really on our side."

"Let's drop it," Marnie said.

Leah's eyes fixed on Jennifer. "You sound like a liberal when you say shit like that."

Jennifer did her best to look bored. "I've been doing this longer."

More cops appeared behind the gate, and the crowd surged. They were either sending a van out or letting one in.

"Fuck the po-lice!" someone chanted.

The gates began to open.

"Fuck the po-lice!" The chant grew louder; hands began clapping in rhythm.

Agents marched out to meet the protesters. Somewhere, one of them had a megaphone, yelling, "Back up! Back up!"

A Mountain Dew bottle arced through the air and landed at an agent's feet. He kicked it to the side as he moved forward.

A drunk man draped in an American flag staggered up front, bellowing at protesters. "Let them through! Back the fuck up, you pussies!" He stopped inches from a woman in her forties.

She took a step back.

He made a sudden movement with his arms as if he was about to hit her and she flinched. Another protester put his body between the two.

Most of the crowd made space for the agents. Jennifer watched the headlights of a van pass over faces as it left the facility.

A few protesters stood their ground. The agents swung their batons. Someone struck an agent with their backpack then tried to get away. They were quickly tackled.

A legal observer peeled through the crowd toward the arrest, but the drunk man body-checked her.

"Hey!" Jennifer yelled. She turned to Leah. "We're helping her, come on." She grabbed Leah's arm and started guiding her toward the legal observer, but Leah pulled back.

Jennifer put her face up to Leah's. "Are you here to do something or just scold me about theory?"

Fear flashed in Leah's eyes before she nodded. "Okay, let's go."

Jennifer grabbed her again and the two ran deeper into the crowd, trailed closely by Mark and Marnie.

A right-wing streamer charged the legal observer. More people crowded in, shoving and yelling.

Jennifer wrapped her arms around the legal observer and spun slowly to remove her from the swarm, then pointed her back to where the arrest was happening. The cops now had three protesters on the ground in cuffs.

A streamer got his camera in Leah's face and she backed away but he followed her. Unable to escape, she took a swing at the camera.

"This Antifa just hit me!" yelled the streamer.

"Fuck you!" someone in the crowd yelled.

Jennifer shoved the streamer and grabbed hold of Leah again. Someone ripped off Jennifer's mask and a blast of cold air hit her face.

Marnie and Mark found them in the chaos and began leading them away.

The drunk man was suddenly in Jennifer's ear. "Be careful not to get fucked out here, bitch. You commie fucking bitch!"

Jennifer shot her elbow back, but some guy had already flung the drunk man to the ground and restrained him.

People collided, tripping over each other, shouting insults.

Jennifer felt Mark's hand on her arm and picked up speed. She noticed his mask had come off in the struggle as well. They retreated from the cluster of bodies.

Pop! Pop! Pop!

The sound of a pellet gun rang across the chaos. Cops swarmed the guy who had helped her. Another agent led the drunk guy away.

Jennifer shifted to turn back, but Marnie firmly gripped her hand and yanked her along. They passed the canopy and continued toward a fence-lined sidewalk that led downtown.

A shuffling sound grew louder behind them.

"Hey! You're gonna pay for that!" An older blonde woman in a zipped-up fleece jacket followed them closely, flanked by other counter-protesters.

"Keep walking," Jennifer said.

A laser darted across the concrete beside Jennifer, then disappeared again. The floodlights faded into the distance as they followed the chain-link fence away from the scene. A streetlight was just up ahead.

"Hey!" the woman called.

There were five of them now. Jennifer's crew picked up their pace and heard someone behind them break into a run.

A woman was approaching up ahead, walking with a bike. She saw them and quietly peeled across the street, head down, and continued on her way.

Leah was panicking. "What do we do?" She halted for a moment, but Mark dragged her forward.

A rush of footsteps. Two chuds ran up beside them and cut them off. One of them reached out to grab Jennifer, backing her into the fence.

"Fuck off, dude!" she yelled and shoved him away.

"Get the fuck away from us!" Mark shouted.

The chud smacked him across the face. Marnie reached out to push him, but he grabbed her sweatshirt sleeve.

"You can't break people's property like that," said the other chud. "We're placing you under citizen's arrest." He grabbed Leah.

"Hey!" came a familiar voice. Chet wedged himself between the two groups. He glanced at Jennifer for a second, then turned to the chuds. "We gotta go back, we're needed up there."

"This bitch just—"

"Come on." Chet grabbed him by the arm and started leading him away.

"What the fuck?" the other one said, incredulous.

"All of us," Chet said. "The officers need our help."

Leah broke into a run and the rest of her crew followed.

After a block, Jennifer realized no one had chased them. She turned back and watched Chet usher the crowd back toward the floodlights.

***

Back at the facility, things had calmed down. The agents made a few arrests and dragged them behind the gates. Half the crowd had dispersed already.

Legal observers had circled up. One streamer was harassing them, but they said some things to him calmly and he gave up and left.

"What the fuck was so important?" Jax demanded.

Chet turned and looked at him stone-faced. "I guess it's all good now. Some of these assholes were trying to de-arrest their friends but it looks like things are under control."

"Things here look absolutely fine," said Tyler. "Meanwhile, you just let three Antifa get away with attacking a journalist."

"We're here to stop Antifa from attacking the facility," Chet replied. "I'm sorry you didn't get to finish harassing those women."

Tyler was looking at Chet with a strange expression. "Harassing?"

Jax and Tyler stood side by side, studying Chet.

He paused, wondering the right thing to say here. "We got them away from the scene. Got them away from the streamers. We did what we needed to do."

"*We* did," said Jax. "You didn't seem so into it."

Chet looked back at Jax, then walked over to the streamer. "You all good, my man? That bitch fuck up your camera or anything?"

The streamer shook his head and pointed his camera at Chet. "Still going strong. Thank you, brother. Say 'what's up' to Truth Nation!"

Chet smiled and flashed the hang loose sign for the stream. "What's good, patriots? Stay vigilant out there, okay?"

***

Chet was just pulling into his driveway when Jennifer's name lit up on his screen.

He turned off the engine and took a deep breath, then answered.

"This is really who you are?" she asked, foregoing a greeting. "Standing up for the modern Gestapo, really?"

He rubbed the back of his neck. "We heard your friends were trying to attack a government building."

"The only attacks that happened tonight were from the police and from you."

Chet sighed. "You all were calmer than I was led to believe you would be."

"You guys chase down women and attack them often?"

"Do you guys beat up journalists a lot?"

"Dude, that's not what happened."

"Your friend has a temper."

Jennifer scoffed loudly on the other line. "What were you guys gonna do to us?"

He didn't know the answer to that. "Some of the guys got riled up and I followed to keep an eye on things. When I saw it was you, I stopped them."

"What if it hadn't been me?"

Chet paused. Something about that question made his head hurt. It was true that Jax and Tyler had been aggressive tonight. Still, they had only come because of Jennifer's side. "Look, some of the guys got worked up. I would have calmed them down either way. You should do the same with your friend; she shouldn't be hitting journalists like that."

There was silence on the line, then Jennifer asked, "Are you okay with them rounding up innocent people like that? ICE? That doesn't remind you of any terrible moments in history?"

"They're deporting criminals. I'm not against all immigrants, but ICE is just trying to stop the cartels."

"Jesus Christ, dude. Do you even read the news?"

"Yeah, I do. Do you?"

"You being inside me and then showing up to help ICE makes me want to vomit. No, it makes me want to jump off a fucking bridge."

"Okay, wow, so last night I was your booty call and now I'm your suicide hotline, too?"

"Fuck you, dude," she said, and hung up the phone.

Chet gazed at the steering wheel, replaying the events of the last twenty-four hours in his head and feeling sick to his stomach. It took several minutes for him to realize he was still sitting in his car.

***

Jennifer sat in her room, face hot. She couldn't believe she had softened herself to this guy for even one moment—he and his friends were ugly and cruel.

Then she thought of the look of concern that had flashed across Chet's face as his eyes met hers.

Marnie knocked on the door.

Jennifer opened it then returned to her bed. "How you feeling, babe?"

Marnie hovered in the doorway with a stoic expression. "What was that tonight?"

Something in her voice made Jennifer feel queasy. She let out a breath and gestured to the bed. "What do you mean?"

Marnie leaned forward as if to accept the invitation, then stopped. "I know that guy."

There was no way she was talking about Chet. Jennifer cocked her head. "What guy?"

Marnie rested against the doorframe. "Jenn, you know what guy. The one who helped us get away."

Whenever she was stressed, Jennifer noticed that a silent room always had an odd hum to it. Like she could hear the lightbulbs buzzing in their fixtures. "You know him?"

"Yes," Marnie replied slowly. She took a step forward. "You do, too."

Jennifer imagined how it would feel if there was some switch she could flick on and lie well. Her body would be calm, face realistically confused, eye contact steady and sure. "I—" She shook her head slowly. "I don't think so."

Marnie tilted her head. "Really?"

Jennifer felt her chest tighten. Her eyes were locked on Marnie's, a death match of sorts where it felt like whoever read the other's mind first won.

"You know," Marnie said as she crossed her arms, "something weird was happening at the gym."

"The gym?"

"The MMA gym. The self-defense class."

Oh fuck. Jennifer opened her mouth then closed it again. She started to raise her hands then dropped them to her lap. "What about it?"

"That guy? Redpill Rambo."

"Who?"

"Your partner from the exercise," Marnie said, clearly exasperated. "You two seemed familiar. And then you both disappeared after class."

Jennifer fought the urge to deny it too quickly.

"Wasn't that him tonight?" Marnie pressed.

"It was dark...maybe."

Marnie's face was red now, her expression a mix of disgust and triumph. Then she laughed humorlessly. "You showed him to me."

Jennifer was feeling very, very stupid. "What?"

"He's phone guy, Jenn."

"Phone guy?"

"You showed me his picture before you went to give back his phone."

Jennifer's mind raced. "I—"

"Phone guy...was gym guy. And he was also there tonight—the guy who let us go. Why did he do that?"

It felt like the blood was draining from Jennifer's head. It was a cold, empty feeling. "Marnie—"

"Were you with him last night? Was he the guy you tried to lie about?"

Jennifer shifted back on her bed and crossed her legs. "You're making a lot of assumptions here."

"Did you fuck a Nazi you met at an anti-Nazi protest?"

"Maybe he's not a Nazi—" Jennifer stopped herself, clocking the expression on Marnie's face.

Marnie made a sound and stepped back toward the doorway. "You are so full of shit."

Jennifer weighed her options. There seemed to be only one. "Okay," she said, rising from her bed and showing her open palms. "I just...I was gonna tell you. I was still processing."

Marnie was staring at her like she'd just ordered a veggie burger but been served beef.

"It just happened somehow," Jennifer admitted, "and I don't know how, and I hate that it happened. It was only once. I don't feel...good."

"How did you—like you *fucked* him fucked him?"

"Marnie—we fucked. I feel gross about it. You win, okay?"

Marnie's face crinkled. "Who are you?"

"Can you let this go for now?"

"Oh, so we're letting things go now?"

The room filled with an uneasy silence. They stood awkwardly, Jennifer not quite facing Marnie and Marnie not quite facing the wall.

Marnie let out a sigh and shook her head. Then she straightened her posture and put her hand on the door. "You don't get to ever give me shit again," she said. "For anything."

Jennifer's head felt cloudy and hot. "Marnie," she said finally, "fuck off."

Marnie hovered a moment, avoiding eye contact. Then she silently walked out of the room.

10

Glass Elevator

Jennifer chose the mall because it was a public place her friends would never be caught dead in. Beyond that, it felt impossible to get too cozy there—it was ugly, fluorescent, depressingly American—a dying relic of a toxic, dying empire.

She sat at a wobbly food court table sipping a matcha smoothie she didn't want while she practiced the script in her head. Keep it clear. Firm. No metaphors.

Chet arrived five minutes late wearing aviators and a hoodie that said *TRUTH ISN'T MEAN, YOU JUST THINK WRONG* in white, blocky letters. He sat across from her, took off the sunglasses, and gestured toward her smoothie. "Yum. Did a plant shop vomit in your cup?"

She smoothed her skirt. "I don't think I said it clearly last night, so I wanted to make sure we are on the same page. What happened was a mistake. I am not okay with anything about you. And I don't want to see you ever again."

Hurt flashed across Chet's face, then quickly hardened into smugness. He exhaled through his nose and leaned back, studying her. "Right into it. No 'how was your day?'"

"I don't want to know about your day. I don't even want to know you."

He looked away. "Cool. That's a very...honest thing to say."

They sat for a moment in the hum of elevator muzak and deep-fryer reverb.

Chet cleared his throat. "You can disagree with me. That's fine. I disagree with you. But I helped you last night. And not because we did it—because I'm a decent guy." He paused. "I know you think I'm dirt. That's fine. Maybe that's why you—"

"A decent guy?"

"You heard me."

"There was nothing decent about any of you guys last night."

Chet pursed his lips and surveyed the food court. "You guys started shit, and I helped you get away."

"We showed up to protest families getting ripped apart. Some Team America asshole threatened me, and that streamer asshole got in Leah's face. That's what you people do."

"We see it different."

"We do." Jennifer scooted her chair back. It screeched and she flinched, then composed herself. "I just wanted to say: No more. That's it. Forget you knew me."

Chet's face was stoic. "You don't want to hook up anymore. That's okay."

"Good."

"But it's weird that you set up a face-to-face instead of just ghosting."

She tilted her head to one side then the other, then nodded in acknowledgement. "I needed you to understand it's done."

"Okay. Heard." He rubbed the back of his neck. "Would never have worked anyway, with the whole raging commie thing. Better this way."

"Sure. Yeah, agreed," Jennifer said. "You are so—not who I date. And it's not gonna happen again, so—"

"Okay, I get it. We won't have sex again. Loud and clear. That it?"

Jennifer sat forward as if to stand, then settled back. "You think this is just sex, but it's not. It's an infection. It's wrong."

Chet laughed once, dryly. "You've got a brain virus. You really do. All of you." He shook his head. "You guys are a mob of brain-dead zombies. And you're so high and mighty about it."

She stood. "Oh my God, dude. Fuck off."

Chet didn't move. "Alrighty then, nice to meet you, Jennifer. Take care."

"Don't text me again. Delete my number."

"Never saved it."

She leaned back but didn't take a step. "This is over. Don't follow me."

He looked at her and stood slowly. "There's only one way down. Don't get your panties in a bunch about it."

They both started toward the elevator, letting shoppers drift between them. It was a glass elevator, the kind people build to look out at something beautiful. All this one did was overlook a run-down consumerist hellscape.

Jennifer pressed the button hard. A two-story Claire's glittered across the atrium. The doors opened and she stepped inside and he stepped in behind her, stationing himself at the opposite end.

The elevator began its descent, then stuttered and screeched to a halt. A button on the pad started blinking red.

"Well, isn't this perfect?" Chet said.

It really was—like the universe was daring Jennifer to fall back into a pit. She wasn't going to take the bait. "I hate you," she muttered.

He looked over. "Good."

Jennifer watched oblivious shoppers bee-line from one store to the next through the glass. Then, she faced him. "You said I had a brain virus."

"I meant it."

Her pulse quickened.

He stepped toward her. "Gonna go start a fire about it?"

The smell of him was familiar and her thighs clenched on instinct.

"You don't know anything about me," she said.

"And you don't know me."

She grabbed the front of his hoodie and pulled his mouth to hers.

They kissed hard, fast, like two people trying to disarm a bomb with their teeth. He shoved a hand under her skirt and she moaned into his mouth.

She half-turned so that her ass was silhouetted by the fluorescent lights outside and locked eyes with him. "Men like you make me wish I was a lesbian."

He spun her around and pressed her into the glass. She let out a gasp as he knelt, mouth finding her from behind. His tongue and fingers pushed her underwear aside and spread her open.

She gripped the metal railing while her forehead pressed into the cool glass. "Oh, *fuck*," she breathed. "You think I don't see through your sad, tough-guy act?"

Chet stood and unzipped without a reply. He pressed against her entrance, thick, ready. With his mouth at her ear, he said, "I think you want to cancel everything but my cock." He pushed inside her with one hungry thrust.

Jennifer cried out.

He grabbed her hips and fucked her hard, deliberate. The sound of his stomach slapping against her ass echoed through the tight space.

The elevator lurched and began moving again. He pressed deeper into her.

The ground floor approached swiftly.

Jennifer opened her eyes just enough to see her reflection. Her mouth was open, eyelashes pressed up against the glass.

This was the last time. She meant it. She may as well enjoy it—she *was* enjoying it. He felt good. A disgusting contradiction, a delicious secret.

She came, trembling. He followed a second later, burying his face in the back of her neck.

The elevator landed and the doors opened and they pulled apart. She yanked her skirt down. He zipped. They didn't speak.

Chet hung back for a moment, letting her walk away briskly before emerging and starting toward the parking garage.

Jennifer passed three mall maps without stopping. After exiting an automatic door, she found herself in the bright light of the sun, clocking the expressions of strangers: laughing, frowning, thinking hard. A guy talking into his AirPods. An older woman with sunglasses and a grimace.

11

You Should See This

When Chet got home from the mall, Roxy was waiting out front. She was wearing a lime-green top and black leggings with a large bag draped casually over one wrist, posture aggressively straight as always.

She'd never dropped by unannounced like this before. For a moment, Chet wondered if someone had seen him at the mall and called her and now Roxy was here to take him to jail. But the question vanished when she lit up and waved eagerly at him, bouncing up on her toes and giving a little wiggle in her hips that should have made him feel horny but instead made him feel tired.

He mustered a smile.

"Hi, babe!" Roxy said. She stepped forward to hug him and he wondered if she'd be able to smell the sex on him. He quickly decided it would be more suspicious to avoid hugging her.

"Hey, you," he said, wrapping his arms around her and sliding his hands down to grab her ass. She pulled back just enough to initiate a kiss and he kissed her back with a closed mouth, patting her butt.

Roxy's eyes flashed over Chet as they pulled apart, her mouth hanging onto the smile a second longer than the rest of her. "Where you been?"

"Errands."

Inside, she pulled him close and kissed him again, hands planted firmly on both shoulders like she had no intention of letting go. "I hear you were a bit of a hero last night."

Chet chuckled nervously. "What do you mean?"

"Well, you know how Tyson Brock and I follow each other on Instagram?"

Chet did know. Tyson was the stuff of alt media legend. He had over a million followers and a few retweets from White House officials. Tyson had first gotten big while covering the Black Lives Matter riots of 2020, when Antifa labeled him a white supremacist and ended up nailing him in the head with what he claimed was a bottle of piss. The incident garnered national news coverage, with one commentator saying it revealed "the dark side of racial justice."

When bystanders insisted it was just Lemon-Lime Gatorade, Tyson doubled down, saying he "knew for a fact it was piss."

"I know about Tyson," Chet answered.

"Well, you met him last night." Roxy's eyes were big like she'd just won the lottery.

"Wow," Chet said, making his best attempt at enthusiasm. "That's...huge." If he was going to fuck left-wing terrorists behind Roxy's back, the least he could do was be supportive of her interests. "I didn't even know."

Roxy shoved him playfully. "He's the guy Antifa attacked. They *hate* him. Really hate him. He DM'd me this morning. Said you helped him out."

Roxy was looking at Chet with glowing eyes and a genuine smile that he wanted to be moved by. Here she was. She loved him. Thought he was a hero, even. The guys liked her. So did the followers. It all made sense.

Except he felt tired and cold, like he was behind glass.

"He wants you to come on his show. He figured out who you were and listened to *Ripped for the Right.*"

"Oh." Chet knew he should keep talking, but something in his brain wasn't firing. His heart was beating loud in his ears, and his vision zoomed in on Roxy.

The excitement slowly drained from her face. "Babe?" she said. "This is everything we've been working toward."

Tyson had filmed parts of what happened last night. What exactly, Chet wasn't sure, but he'd had Chet say hi to the stream. And he'd maybe caught some of Jennifer.

"Of course. I just..." He took a step back and glanced around his apartment. The blinds were drawn, and they hadn't turned the lights on, leaving the space unnaturally dark for the afternoon. Nauseating almost. Or maybe *he* was nauseous. He needed a moment to himself. "I'll be right back." He took a cautious step then did a sharp heel turn and headed to the bathroom. "I think I had something funny for lunch."

Chet felt Roxy's eyes on him as he stepped into the bathroom and closed the door. His heart was pounding in his ears. He took some deep breaths but it didn't help. Lifting the lid of the toilet, he wondered if he might hurl, but didn't, so he pulled his pants down and took a seat.

That guy was Tyson Brock? He was kind of an asshole. Jennifer's friend had been a bitch for hitting his stuff, but he had gotten aggressive with them first.

He stared at the floor. Grime and dust. Hadn't cleaned in a bit. Not since Jennifer was here. He did a quick scan for any long, brown hairs but didn't see any.

Chet took out his phone and went to Tyson's Twitter. His last post went up a few hours ago. Footage from last night. He watched with the sound off. Tyson had the camera on Jennifer and her friend. Then the friend took a swing and the video cut to black for a moment. At the end, a closing snippet of Jennifer and her friend walking away, and Jax ripping off Jennifer's mask.

Chet clicked to expand the text block:

Can you help me identify the paid protesters who assaulted me?

Last night, I went to the ICE facility to expose Antifa's continued assault on law enforcement. What I saw changed everything. While patriots showed up with flags to thank our federal law enforcement officers, paid anarchists showed up in all black and stormed the gate. The agents handled the situation with the utmost professionalism but...

Roxy knocked on the door. "Babe, are you okay?"

Chet's eyes scanned to the bottom.

These are the women who attacked me. Let's make them famous. Can you help me identify who they are?

Fifty-four comments.

"All good," Chet called through the door. "I'll be out soon."

He should warn her. Tyson Brock going after her was not a good situation. He wondered if she had blocked him. If she had, he wasn't sure how to reach her.

He hit the share button, sent the tweet to Jennifer, and typed *Hey, you should see this.*

He held his breath until it showed as delivered.

***

When Jennifer got home from the mall, she took a very long shower.

At one point, Marnie knocked and said she needed to pee.

"Then come do it," said Jennifer, unable to make her voice sound friendly.

Marnie opened the door and did her business in stony silence. She flushed and ran the tap. "Weird time of day to shower," she said, then left again.

Jennifer stood there way longer after that without moving. The warm water gathered in her hair and cascaded down her back.

She closed her eyes and imagined stepping out of the shower as a kind of reset. The Chet thing had happened, sure. A few times. Now it was done. She'd said it was done and meant it. The elevator sex didn't change that. When she stepped out, she would go back to normal. She wasn't a Nazi fucker. It had just been a fluke and now it was done. If anything, she'd tried it and knew it wasn't who she was. She was more certain of it now, if anything.

In fact, she was more committed to the cause than she had been before.

She stepped out and hovered in the bathroom. The air was thick and wet. The mirror was fogged. She could see faint hints of her reflection behind a layer of mist.

She dried herself absent-mindedly, then wrapped a towel in her hair and opened the door.

Leah was crying on the couch, with Marnie consoling her. Her face was puffy and red.

Jennifer stood there a moment, droplets landing on the floor beneath her. "Hey," she said. "Are you okay?"

Marnie looked up. "There's a video of last night." Her demeanor had softened in a way that made Jennifer uneasy. "The guy that got in Leah's face posted the footage. You're in it, too."

Jennifer moved across the room and sat next to Leah. "Okay, so..."

"It's that Nazi asshole," said Leah. "Piss Bottle Guy. Do you remember Piss Bottle Guy?"

Jennifer nodded. She did remember Piss Bottle Guy.

This all seemed unreal. Part of her felt like she should be panicking, but she wasn't quite sure she understood enough to panic.

"He's trying to doxx you two." Marnie's tone was apologetic.

A draft hit Jennifer's bare shoulders, and she shivered. "Can I have someone's phone?"

Leah took a deep breath and grabbed her phone off the table then held it out to Jennifer without looking at her.

The post was already pulled up. Sixty-eight comments. Some screengrabs. A blurry still of Jennifer, right after her mask was ripped off. Some folks had tagged random brunette OnlyFans models. The rest were the typical mix of marriage proposals and physical threats, save for some left-wingers posting bottle emojis.

"Well, it doesn't look like anyone has identified us," Jennifer said, glancing at Marnie.

"Do you think they will?" asked Leah.

Marnie watched Jennifer intently.

"No," Jennifer said, more confidently than she felt. "They won't."

Leah's hands were clasped in her lap, one thumb stroking the palm of her other hand. "If this gets back to my school, I don't know what that means for me or my class." She stared into space a moment then turned to Jennifer. "They got your mask off. I'm sorry they got your mask off."

They had gotten her mask off. There it was—her face on Twitter.

"It's okay," Jennifer said. "It'll be okay."

"I feel like it's my fault."

Marnie shook her head.

"It's not," said Jennifer. "That streamer attacked you. That's not your fault. And they don't have your face."

"Will they find you, though? They have yours..."

"No," said Jennifer.

Leah glanced back at Marnie then turned to Jennifer. "Do any of the Nazis know who you are?"

Leah's brown, dull eyes were bloodshot and pleading.

Jennifer took a breath, studying Leah for a moment. Then she looked at Marnie, who was silent, eyes fixed on Jennifer. "No," said Jennifer. She cleared her throat. "None of them know me."

***

After Leah left, Jennifer went to her room to dress and check her phone.

Dev had texted: *You doing okay? Headed over.*

Chet had sent her the link to Tyson's video.

She wasn't sure if there was a head game in there, or if he was showing genuine concern. She decided it didn't really matter and responded *never contact me again* then opened the video to check the comment section again. No one had identified them yet. She let out a long, slow exhale. Then she opened Dev's text and liked it.

Jennifer emerged from her room to find Marnie at the kitchen table, drinking a glass of wine and staring into space. When she heard Jennifer, she looked up.

Jennifer started to raise her hand to give an awkward wave, then stopped. "Dev's coming over," she said.

"Okay." Marnie mustered a gentle smile. "How are you feeling?"

Jennifer moved as if to join at the table, then stopped. "Weird. I don't know. It sucks."

"It does." Marnie patted the tabletop.

Jennifer sank into the chair next to Marnie. She rested her hands on the table. It felt unnatural. She dropped them to her sides. "I ended it with Chet," she said. "It's over."

Marnie slid her glass across the table.

Jennifer took a sip.

"Are you okay?" Marnie asked.

"I'll be fine."

Marnie scooted her chair closer. "I'm sorry things have been weird between us," she said, scanning Jennifer. "I just don't—I just don't understand what's going on with you."

Jennifer rested a hand on the table, gazing at it a moment, then looked up at Marnie. "I'm sorry, too."

"Are we still...like, I don't even know if you like me anymore. Do you hate me?"

"No. I don't hate you."

Marnie pushed a strand behind her ear slowly. "Are you mad at me?"

Jennifer took a deep breath and held it in a few seconds, then exhaled. "A little. Are you mad at me?"

"I am kind of. But mostly I'm scared for you."

"I'm scared, too."

"I'm scared that Chet knows where we live. I'm not trying to be a bitch, I just really don't understand why you did that."

Jennifer felt herself collapsing inward in the chair. "He doesn't know where I live. And it's done, truly. We don't have to think about it anymore."

"Promise?"

Jennifer felt a flash of hurt. "Yes."

Marnie cautiously reached across the table and took the glass back. "How did he...take it?" Marnie was being genuine.

Jennifer cautiously grinned and Marnie grinned a bit, too. "He said I had a brain virus."

Marnie's lip quivered a bit. "Like...'Soros brain virus'?"

That got a laugh out of Jennifer. "Oh, yeah. He's mentioned Soros a couple times."

Marnie made an "eeee" sound and set the glass down, giggling and putting her free hand up to her mouth.

Knock, knock, knock.

They both flinched.

"It's probably Dev," said Jennifer. She stood to open it, then hovered at the table and called him from her phone, just to make sure.

It was Dev. Jennifer gave Marnie an awkward nod then shuffled to the door, pausing to take a deep breath before letting him in.

Dev entered, bearing a Hershey's milk chocolate bar. "I know you love chocolate," he said, placing it tentatively in her hand, like he was suddenly unsure of himself.

She loved dark chocolate. But this was sweet of him.

"This is so unfair for you, I'm sorry," Dev said. He took her hand in his and squeezed it. "You should do a digital security cleanse. I can help you."

"Okay," Jennifer said. "Thanks."

Dev shuffled to the kitchen and opened the fridge. "Do you use *DuckDuck-Go*?"

Later, they were kissing in bed when Dev started to climb on top of her and she stopped him. "I'm sorry can we—I don't think I want to tonight. Is that okay?"

"Yeah," he said. He moved back slowly, keeping eye contact. "Just, whatever you need, okay? I just want you to be okay."

She studied him. For a second she wanted to tell him everything. "Will you just hold me?"

"Of course."

Jennifer rolled away and let Dev wrap his arms around her, pulling his hand in tight to her chest. She felt herself trembling and tried not to. She could hear the humming of the light fixtures, feel his warm breath on her neck. The image of Tyson's post was clear in her mind—countless eyes on her.

"Dev?"

"Yeah?"

She readjusted her head on the pillow. She shouldn't be putting him through this. Or Marnie. Or Leah.

"I'm scared," she said.

He nudged her back with his forehead. "I know," he said. "I'm sorry."

12

TruthSmash

Jennifer was brushing her teeth the next day when Marnie knocked on the door and shoved her phone into Jennifer's hands.

"You need to find a new place to live," she said, then walked away.

Baffled, Jennifer looked at the phone. It was a video someone had posted yesterday from inside the mall. An elevator descending. Two figures coming into view. Her, bent forward against the glass. Him, thrusting from behind.

What the actual fuck.

A popular gender studies meme account had posted it with the caption: *Yes, he's trash. But also: Have you seen his arms?? Discuss.* The comments were immediate and spiraling.

She played it again and paused toward the end. It was grainy, but in those final frames there was no mistake who they both were.

Jennifer spat in the sink like she was exorcising something, then stormed into the living room calling Marnie's name.

Dev was in the kitchen, shirtless, making something in a mason jar. He looked up. "Can we talk?"

"One second. Marnie!" She headed to Marnie's room and knocked.

"Fuck off!" Marnie's voice came through the door.

Dev appeared behind her in the hall. "This feels like a huge and very public breach of trust."

"Dev, I'm sorry, we can talk about this, but first I need to chat with Marnie—"

"There's nothing else to say!"

Jennifer banged on the door again. "Can we calm the fuck down, please?"

Dev was crying now and mashing chia seeds with a spoon. "I'm having a hard time processing this."

Marnie opened the door. "Jennifer, you're still fucking this guy? After everything that happened?"

"You know I believe in consensual non-monogamy but to hide it from me?" Dev said.

Jennifer turned back to Dev. "This isn't about you." She took a step toward Marnie who stepped forward to block her.

"You have no fucking boundaries! First you fuck a fascist, now what—you're gonna scope out my room and fuck him on my bed?"

Behind her, Dev was still talking. "Did he even go down on you? Did he? That's a major issue among non-enlightened men."

"Marnie, I met him there to break up with him. It's done. That was the last time."

Marnie snorted. "That's what you said the other time!"

Dev let out another sob. "There was another time?"

"Marnie, we can talk this out. I can fix this."

"How the fuck do you fix this? It's everywhere, Jenn. Your face is everywhere. And now I'm not safe in my own fucking home." Marnie's phone rang. "It's Leah." She tried to close the door, but Jennifer jammed a foot in the doorway.

Dev put a hand on Jennifer's shoulder. "Please—"

Jennifer swatted him away while struggling to keep her foot lodged in the doorframe as Marnie, who was on the phone now, leaned her body against the door to force it closed. "No, I didn't know... Yes, obviously I think it's problematic!"

Dev dropped his mason jar and chia seeds went everywhere.

Jennifer turned to look and heard Marnie's door slam behind her.

She looked at Dev. He had searching eyes and swollen cheeks. "Are you in love with him?"

Jennifer let out a sigh. "No."

"You hesitated."

"Because it's a stupid question."

"What about me?"

Jennifer put her hand over her face. "Dev, we broke up like a year ago."

Dev hovered a moment, shoulders collapsing inward like a canopy after a street fair, then he clutched his phone to his chest. "Okay." He shuffled into the bathroom and shut the door.

Jennifer stood in the hall, taking in the silence. Then she grabbed a rag from the kitchen and started scraping chia seeds out of the rug.

***

Chet recorded the interview with Tyson from his living room, with Roxy perched eagerly just out of frame.

They had spent all morning getting the lighting just right, using Chet's ring light and both of hers.

Chet's phone kept buzzing, which irritated Roxy and made him feel on edge, so he put it on airplane mode.

Roxy was a nervous wreck, at one point reprimanding him for the location of his windows, as if he had placed them there personally.

Chet hadn't expected everything to happen so fast and still wasn't sure he wanted to do the interview. But the previous night, Jennifer had responded to his text with "never contact me again," and after an hour watching TV with Roxy—quietly feeling like there was a bus on his chest—Chet initiated some of the best sex they'd ever had, blurting out that he wanted to go on the podcast right before he came.

Now, it was one minute before showtime.

Roxy pulled up the link Tyson emailed her and asked Chet to change his shirt for the third time. "This one will make your eyes pop more, promise."

Chet begrudgingly took off the black muscle tank he'd been wearing and put on the navy-blue muscle tank Roxy was offering.

She smoothed his hair and then whispered into his ear, "I might end up just blowing you right here. Try not to let it show."

Tyson's podcast was called *TruthSmash* and the opening music sounded custom made. He appeared before a greenscreen with a graphic of a globe composed of ones and zeroes. "Okay, truthspeakers, today we have a guy whose work I have admired for a long time, but we just met for the first time a few days ago. Chet, say hello to Truth Nation!"

Chet looked at his frame. It looked...weak compared to Tyson's. "What's up, Truth Nation? Tyson, my man, it's great to be here."

"So, a lot of folks know this story, but for those who don't, let's catch 'em up. You and I met a few nights ago when some Antifa soldiers were trying to storm a government building and kill police. I was there with my camera to document the truth—" Tyson's audio engineer cued the sound of a whip, followed by a "Truth Nation" vocal tag "—and you were there—now help me out here, 'cause this is what I think is so amazing: You and your boys were there to stand up to these motherfuckers and show them that Americans support ICE. Is that right?"

In his peripheral, Chet saw Roxy punch the air and nod enthusiastically.

Chet swallowed. "We heard there was gonna be a major...problem, and we're not the type of guys to let that kinda thing fly."

Roxy mimed clapping her hands.

"That's awesome, Chet. That's what's so important these days with Antifa terrorizing our cities—it's gonna take people like us, right? Everyday Americans standing up and saying 'enough is enough'. Now, we have a video of what went down that night. Let's take a look."

The same clip Tyson had posted the day prior started to play. There was Jennifer. Chet's stomach sank.

Roxy flashed a thumbs up.

"Now, Chet, what's your take on this? Because we're both independent media guys, right? You've got your pod, too, which we're gonna get more into later but, as a fellow media guy: What do you think of what Antifa is doing? Attacking the independent press? I mean, we're the only guys out there telling the truth."

In the corner of the screen, a red indicator light was blinking. The chat was full of running commentary, and thousands of people were tuning in live.

Chet was uncomfortably aware of how much dead airtime had passed since Tyson finished his question. "Well... The way I look at it...they shouldn't be rioting—"

"Exactly," Tyson cut in. "And that's what we saw that night, unfortunately. Another violent riot. Now when you stepped in and chased those Antifa down who attacked me—And by the way, I've asked the public for help identifying them. I know a lot of people out there want to stand up to these thugs. But that night, you and your buddies were there, and you *did* stand up to them. What was going through your head?"

That night, Chet had been watching for any sign of the type of violence that got him showing up to fight Antifa—fires getting started, officers getting stuff thrown at them, windows getting smashed. Chet hadn't seen anything like that. He'd seen the officers being pretty assertive with protesters who were blocking the road. That was fine, they were the professionals.

He hadn't really seen what started the clash between Tyson and Jennifer's friends. But all of a sudden, there she was, and she was trying to get away, and then Jax and Tyler were chasing her. So Chet followed.

The producer's voice came through Chet's headphones. "Hey, guys, we're gonna need to run some pre-taped stuff here for just a few minutes, okay?"

Unsure what to do or say, Chet smiled awkwardly.

Tyson jumped in. "Okay, guys. We have some videos to play, but we'll be right back."

B-roll of some old street brawl started playing. "Hey, Chet, you're doing great. Me and Brendan are gonna huddle for a sec, but don't go anywhere, okay?"

"Sounds good, man. I'll be here."

Tyson's video feed cut to black.

Chet looked at Roxy and she raised her hands in question.

"They cut to break," Chet explained. "We'll go back on in a bit."

She leaned in and kissed him hard. "You're doing so good, baby. So good!"

"Thanks."

Roxy ran a hand up his leg and lowered her head, looking up at him with doe eyes. "Can you do me a favor?"

"Yeah?"

"Mention me? I think it will be good for your profile if people know there's a whole media universe here. Don't you think?"

Dazed, Chet nodded. "All right."

The producer's voice was in his ear again. "Ready, Chet?"

"Yeah."

Tyson's camera turned back on. "Okay, we are back and we have some breaking news. This is a TruthSmash exclusive and Chet, I am so glad you are here with us today. Now, we have just gotten our hands on a video that's breaking records on PatriotNet. Chet, we're gonna roll the tape and then we'll have you tell us your thoughts, okay?"

It probably took Chet longer than it should have to recognize himself in the elevator video. It was pretty grainy at first, but his first thought was that the woman looked like Jennifer. Then he realized it was Jennifer, and that was him thrusting into her from behind. The video stopped on a freeze frame.

His ears were ringing. Chet heard Tyson say something, but the sound was muffled.

Roxy's face was frozen in horror. She turned to look at him, but her face didn't change.

The red indicator light was still blinking. Comments in the feed were stacking at a disorienting speed.

He wondered for a second if this was a bad dream.

"Chet," came Tyson's voice again. "Are you still with us? Can you hear me?"

"What... What was that?"

Roxy had sunk back in her chair now, staring into space.

"Well that, my friend, appears to be you getting it on in a shopping mall. What listeners have been messaging us about, though, is that woman you're getting it on with. She looks familiar, doesn't she? Let's review the tape."

The feed went into a split screen. The elevator video was frozen on a still of Jennifer. In the other screen, the video from the ICE facility was playing. The moment Jennifer's mask was ripped off. Over and over and over.

"Now, that seems to be the same Antifa who attacked me. The one you chased off. So, what I think Truth Nation would love to hear is: how did you two end up in an elevator doing the dirty?"

Chet considered answering. In his video feed, he could see the blood had drained from his face. He struggled to breathe.

Roxy stood and hovered unnaturally in the kitchen.

"By the way, I'm still looking for help identifying those two women. Looks like you might know who they are, though. Is that right?"

"Tyson," Chet started. Thousands of viewers. "I think you should fuck off." Then he ended his broadcast and shut the laptop.

Chet turned in his seat to look at Roxy. Her face was a shade of red he'd never seen before.

"Is this a PSYOP?" she demanded. "Or some kind of prank?"

Chet didn't answer.

"Did you get deepfaked?"

He shook his head.

She made a noise you might hear during an exorcism and lurched, chucking her phone at him. "You are such a fucking cuck!"

He dodged the phone and stood, hands out in front of him. "Babe, let's just calm down. We can talk about this."

"Calm down?" She looked at him in disbelief. "This ruins *everything*. Do you know what this makes me look like? And *you*. Who the fuck even are you? Some kind of double agent?"

Chet looked at her helplessly.

Roxy paced the kitchen. "I *defended* you in my carnivore group chat."

He didn't know what that meant.

Roxy was in tears now. "Is this about that time you asked me to do butt stuff and I called you a queer?"

Chet flinched. "You know that was a joke."

"Are you into her?"

He didn't answer.

Roxy let out a sob and stormed to the bathroom.

At a loss for what to do, Chet walked out the front door and got in his car. He took his phone off airplane mode and watched the notifications flood in. Dozens of messages, including one from his cousin in Michigan that just said *nice* and another from a podcast sponsor warning him this wasn't brand-aligned.

He opened Jennifer's contact and looked at it. Eventually, he put the phone down and started the car.

PART TWO

13

Hobby Lobby

At sunset, the sky over the Hobby Lobby was a deep orange and street-lamps buzzed over the half-full lot.

Jennifer tried to look casual as she walked, scanning the rows of cars until she found Chet's Tacoma. She climbed inside and dropped a duffel bag at her feet.

"Well," Chet said once she closed the door, "it's a bit of a situation out there."

He looked like he hadn't changed clothes in a while, and his eyes had bags under them. Jennifer was relieved to see him in one piece, which only made her feel annoyed with herself.

She sniffed. "Why the fuck would you go on that guy's podcast?"

He reached out to touch her but stopped when she leaned back. "I don't know," he replied. "It was supposed to help boost my podcast. And Roxy really wanted me to." Chet snuck a glance at her before looking away again. "And you made it pretty clear you didn't want anything to do with me."

"So, it's Roxy's fault." She paused. "Or my fault?"

Chet was gazing out the windshield. "I'm just telling you what happened."

She let out a breath and sank lower in her seat. "Were you gonna help him doxx me?"

"No. I tipped you off. Remember?"

"Maybe you tipped me off to scare me into talking to you again."

"That's not who I am."

Jennifer studied his face. A month ago, the thought of getting into a car with this guy would have scared her shitless. "You keep saying that. I don't understand who you think you are."

He was quiet a moment. "Okay," he said.

"That's all you got?"

He shifted, resting his left arm on the wheel. "*You* called me."

That was true. She hadn't planned on it, but her friends had shown up to help Marnie evict her, and when she called Dev, he didn't answer. After a while, it occurred to her that the only person that might still be concerned about her situation was Chet. The realization made her feel guilty in an empty way.

"Your Nazi buddies doxxed me," she said.

Chet avoided eye contact.

For some reason, that made her feel safer, like he had a sense of shame.

He bit his lip and nodded in concession. "Tyson doxxed me, too."

"You doxxed yourself by going on his fucking podcast."

Chet squinted his eyes as if thinking. After a moment, he said, "Okay."

"And you didn't call me after."

"You told me not to contact you again."

She let out an exasperated laugh. "So, you recorded a podcast with the guy who wants to get me killed?"

Chet remained unnaturally still. "I wish I hadn't done that."

"Because there were consequences for you," said Jennifer. "Not because you care about me."

He started to reach out again but stopped himself, instead letting his hand rest on the parking brake. "I do care about you," he said. "It didn't feel good when you said you wanted to end things. It didn't sit right."

"Well, now your friends are looking for me. Did you bring them with you?"

"Why would you come here if you thought I had them with me?"

Jennifer shrugged. He had a point.

Chet cleared his throat. "I assumed if you were asking to meet up, that meant we were good."

"Jury's still out."

He leaned his head against the headrest. "You talk like I'm this dangerous asshole," he said finally, "but you don't act like you really think I am."

"You went on a podcast with a guy who doxxed me. Like the *same* day he doxxed me."

"They're after me, too," he reminded her. "They think I was a double agent or something. A secret Antifa. 'Cause of you."

"'Cause of me?"

"Yeah, because I fucked you."

She made an incredulous noise.

Chet leaned toward her, and she felt a dull buzzing in her head. "You don't act like you think I'm like them," he said.

"Oh, so you're not like them?"

He paused like he was thinking about that for the first time. "I don't know. They don't want me now. I'm fucked." He sighed heavily. "And I'm sorry they're being creeps to you, but believe me, these guys would be even rougher with me."

"Aw," Jennifer taunted, "I'm sorry your Nazi friends don't think you're Nazi enough, so now they want to hurt you instead of just hurting immigrants and women."

"Well," he said, "I'm sorry your commie friends found out you're straight."

The corner of Jennifer's mouth twitched. She noticed herself feeling charmed, which was mortifying but familiar. Silently, she watched a car back out of its spot.

When she looked at Chet, he was still watching her. "I got kicked out of my place," she said. "Marnie told me to leave, and I said I wouldn't, and then all our friends came and stood in my living room chanting 'Liberate this house! Liberate this house!'"

Chet's face scrunched into a mix of empathy and confusion. "What does that...mean?"

She shrugged. "Nothing. Just...some self-righteous lefty bullshit."

Their eyes met. Then Chet started laughing and she did, too.

"They're supposed to hate evictions," Jennifer added. The more she laughed, the funnier it was.

Chet was grinning, and somehow they had both leaned closer. His eyes darted out the window then back to her eyes and he said, "Someone on PatriotNet edited my orgasm face onto a bald eagle."

"Really?"

"Yes."

She planted a hand on his leg. "Show me."

With a conspiratorial smirk, he pulled up the thread titled *CROSS-IDEO-LOGICAL CUCKHOLE* and scrolled the comments. There it was: a blurry screengrab of Chet's face mid-orgasm over an AI-generated bald eagle in front of an American flag.

Jennifer put a hand over her mouth. "You do look like that when you come."

Chet threw his head back and let out a full belly laugh.

She wiped her eyes. "Do I look stupid when I come?"

"No, you look good." He paused. "You get these pouty lips and your eyes get squinty." He was smiling, but then his face dropped like he was embar-rassed.

It was sweet, what he had just said. He still wouldn't look at her, so she turned her attention back to the phone. The pinned message on the thread read, *We locate. We livestream. We cleanse.* In the comments, there was a blurry image of her from a protest three years ago, yelling into a megaphone.

Someone had drawn crosshairs over her mouth.

She lingered on the image a moment, feeling her chest tighten, then kept scrolling. "My friends are assholes, but yours are…" She held up the phone to show him a comment:

Gas Cuck Beefwell.

Chet looked at it, then took a deep breath through his nose. "I know. Things are out of hand."

"Some Antifascist blog said I was an undercover Nazi."

"I know."

A van pulled up next to them and parked. Three men got out. Chet scanned their faces and Jennifer kept her eyes on him, searching for any sign of recognition. The men walked toward the store.

Jennifer watched them until they disappeared. "What do you think you'll do?"

"I don't know. I don't think we can stay here right now."

She side-eyed him. "We?"

Chet sniffed and shifted in his seat to face her straight on. "I'm getting the fuck out of here," he said. "You should, too. If you meant those things at the mall, and you want to do your own thing, that's fine, but we should both leave town for a while."

Jennifer leaned her forehead against the glass. "I have nowhere to go," she admitted. "You got somewhere?"

He exhaled. "I don't know."

They sat in silence for a moment. Outside, a mother with two young children in tow returned to her minivan with a shopping bag. She set the bag down and started fumbling with a car seat.

Chet cleared his throat. "I think I know a place we'd probably be all right. But it's...weird."

Jennifer wasn't sure she wanted to know, but curiosity won out. "Weird how?"

"It's this sort of...apolitical commune. Granola types. Preppers but in a cucked way."

"Like a cult?"

"I thought you people liked communes."

This was...not what she had expected. She studied him quizzically. "Why do you know them?"

"I don't really know them, I just know *of* them. They sponsored the raw milk bar at a Wim Hof seminar I went to."

She decided not to dwell on that. "Are they Nazis?"

"Definitely not. They don't do ideologies."

"But are they racist?"

"They say they don't see race."

"So, you discussed it?"

Chet sighed. "Look, they aren't really on the grid. If anyone hasn't seen the video, it's them."

Jennifer frowned.

"You got somewhere better?"

A beat. "Chet, I mean it. Can I trust you?"

Chet looked her in the eyes. "Yes." He paused, then added, "Are you gonna fuck me over?"

She shook her head.

They sat in silence a moment, taking it in. Then he extended a hand. "Same team?"

It hovered there, firm and familiar. The threshold she must cross in order to reach out and shake his hand felt much vaster than the one she'd crossed by hooking up with him in the bathroom of a gym and the bathroom of his house and then later in a shopping mall.

She looked at Chet's face. His expression was soft, eyes anxious with antic-ipation.

She reached over and shook.

14

In the Enemy's Kitchen

Jennifer gazed out the window for long stretches of the drive. The scenery shifted from industrial lots to rolling hills before they lifted off into the mountains.

After about an hour, Chet cleared his throat and mumbled something about Jennifer missing work.

She lifted her shoulders. "I don't feel safe going back right now anyway."

"Aren't you worried about money?"

She thought about it. "A little bit, but I'm more worried about safety." She sighed and studied his profile a moment. "How about you?" she asked.

"Well, my podcast is fucked, so..." He glanced at her as if he felt embarrassed by that.

In the dark, the mountains broke long enough to reveal moonlight shimmering off water in the distance.

"How much longer do we have?" Jennifer asked.

Chet squinted his eyes. "Maybe three hours?"

"Are we gonna need to find a motel?"

"There's a town just up the road," Chet said. "We can find one there."

Out the window, there were no signs or turnouts. Jennifer studied Chet. "Do you know this area?"

"Sort of," he said, checking the odometer.

The hum of tires grew louder as the asphalt grew more ragged.

Chet turned his head toward her. "So, you're a nurse, right?"

"What's that?"

"Aren't you a nurse?"

She studied his outline. "Yeah."

"And so, the hospital... Do they pay you to go be a nurse at protests?"

Jennifer watched him, wondering if he was joking, but quickly realized he was not. "I volunteer my time. Those things matter. Your friends attack people there. And so do the cops. I go to those things to patch people up."

Chet made a thinking sound and kept his eyes on the road.

She cleared her throat. "I got attacked at one of those things. A few months ago."

Chet looked at her. "Really? Were you okay?"

"I got kicked in the ribs. No injuries. Just scary."

Chet sat with that a moment. "What were you—"

"What was I doing to deserve it?"

A beat.

"I didn't mean it like that."

Jennifer met his gaze. "Yes, you did." A slight headache was building in her temples, and she wondered how much water she'd had to drink. "I was treating someone who got bear maced by one of your guys."

He nodded, keeping his eyes fixed forward. "I'm sorry they did that to you."

"Would you have done it, too?"

"Really? That's not me."

She wanted to believe him.

"My position has always been that we don't attack people," he continued. "If people attack us, we defend ourselves. That's it."

"Your buddies don't agree, then. Do they?"

"We didn't always see eye to eye. Some of the guys wanted to be more...proactive, maybe."

Headlights passed, going the other way. The first car Jennifer had seen in a while. "Why don't you agree with them?"

Chet paused. "I figured violence and destruction was supposed to be your guys' thing."

"So you never started anything with a protester?"

"In the early days, a little maybe. It's been a while." He readjusted his grip on the wheel and faced her. "What about you? You ever go around throwing things at cops and setting fires?"

Jennifer shook her head. "We show up to oppose Nazis when they march," she said. "We protest outside of police buildings and ICE detention centers. Maybe a few people would start fights or set fires every now and then. I don't think it compares to the violence of the state or the far right. But I also don't feel like it's good. And it doesn't help the left win people over."

"Hmm."

"Still," she added, "property damage isn't as bad as someone getting shot or beat up just for how they look or talk."

Chet stayed silent. A few moments later, without warning, he peeled off to the shoulder and stopped the car.

Jennifer's back tensed and she reached her right hand down for a weapon she didn't have.

He caught her eyes. "I just need to stretch my legs." He got out and popped his back. Then he wandered up to the front of the car, dropped, and started doing pushups. For a while, the only sounds were his grunts and the chirping of crickets.

Jennifer stepped out of the car and leaned against the hood to watch him. "Are we...where you grew up or something?"

Chet dropped to a kneel, wiping his forehead with his sleeve. "Kind of. It just happens to be on the way to where we're going."

"Why didn't you say something?"

He shrugged.

Jennifer shivered. "You're gonna need to sleep. We're both gonna need to sleep."

Chet lingered on the ground. "We could…"

Jennifer waited.

"My parents' house is about forty minutes away."

She crossed her arms and studied him. "You're taking me to meet your parents?"

He stood and gazed into the woods. "I'm taking us to an apolitical living hub," he said finally. "But my parents' house is close by. And there's a bed."

***

Chet's parents' house was in an aging suburb with run-down pickup trucks and *Veterans for Christ* lawn signs in front yards. Jennifer noticed Chet stealing glances at her face as she took it all in.

"Did you grow up in a place like this?" he asked.

She paused a moment. "Seattle area. We would spend summers closer to the lake, though."

"Are your folks still there?"

"Yeah," she said. "I don't really talk to them much."

He gave a sheepish grin. "Parents."

Chet's mom opened the door wearing a moth-eaten cardigan and pearl studs. "My goodness," she said. "We were starting to think you were dead."

"Passing through," Chet said. "Figured we should stop in. I, uh—I don't want to argue about the state of the world this time."

She nodded and then put out one arm for a hug.

"This is Jennifer," Chet said, reaching out as if to put a hand on Jennifer's shoulder.

Chet's mom looked her up and down. "I'm Sandy." She flashed an effortful smile. "You must be the one who made him get a haircut."

***

Chet's father made a brief appearance to say stilted hellos then spent the rest of the evening kicked back with a heating pad on a La-Z-Boy in the sitting room, drinking one Coors Light after another and staring at old UFC fight reruns.

Sandy set out reheated lasagna and wine from a bottle that had a small American flag on the label. She and Chet kept the conversation mostly surface-level—updates about the neighbors, asking after old classmates. Chet skillfully evaded questions about his own life or Jennifer's, offering short, misleading but not dishonest answers, then excused himself after dessert, claiming a migraine.

"I can show you the room," Chet said, but Jennifer waved him off, saying she'd be in soon and should help clean.

"Don't worry about any of this," Sandy said. "I mean it. You're our guest."

Jennifer lingered as Sandy stacked dishes in the sink. The kitchen was small and the counters were crowded with snacks and envelopes. The fridge door was covered with religious magnets and several old family photos.

Chet had a shy, sweet smile as a boy. His father had been handsome when he was younger but didn't really smile in pictures. In the most recent photo Jennifer could find, Chet looked about twelve.

Sandy was loading the dishwasher when she looked at Jennifer and asked, "So, are you...like him?"

The question caught her off guard. "I... What do you mean?"

"The conspiracies, the fights..." She wandered to the sink and started scrubbing a pan. "You don't seem like you are."

Jennifer studied Sandy's profile carefully. "We disagree on a lot."

"That's healthy," Sandy said. "I shouldn't have said anything,"

The room fell silent except for the ticking of an old-school clock. At one point, Sandy caught Jennifer looking at her and gave a pained smile. Jennifer, who had instinctually looked away, returned her gaze, aware of the awkward manners she was displaying, and course-corrected by smiling back.

"And where'd you grow up, Jennifer?"

"Seattle."

"Beautiful area, isn't it?"

A soap bubble drifted up from the sink and settled on Sandy's apron.

Jennifer smiled politely. "It is."

"Parents still live there?"

"They do."

Sandy set the pan down and made a funny face to herself. "We don't think like he does, if you're wondering." She let out a nervous laugh as she gathered utensils from the sink. "We're just...normal, really. Traditional. Not..."

Jennifer shook her head. "I wasn't..."

Sandy nodded. "Okay," she said. "I'm sorry I'm acting strange. I just haven't seen him in a while."

Jennifer hesitated, then said, "When did he get into all of that?"

"Hard to say," Sandy said thoughtfully, wiping her hands on her apron. "You know, growing up, he was like any boy. A bit sensitive, maybe. Then... I don't know. Middle school. Football. His dad's accident." She pushed the rack into the machine and closed the door. "After school was rough. Finding work was rough—for all of us. There was something that never really quite clicked."

Jennifer looked down. The linoleum pattern was nagging in its familiarity. "Do you think he'll..."

Sandy pressed her lips together. "We don't hear much from him," she said. "What do you think?"

"I don't know," said Jennifer. She was blushing. "Maybe I don't really know what I'm asking."

A silence hung between them again. Sandy's face softened. "Would you like some tea?"

Jennifer shook her head. "Thank you."

Sandy glanced toward the sitting room and leaned against the sink. "You know, at my age, you start to notice how many ways you can lose someone. It never really goes back to how it was."

Jennifer stayed silent, fiddling with her necklace.

Sandy wandered over to the table and picked up the wine bottle to see how much was left. "You're very pretty. And you seem nice." She drained the remaining wine into her glass.

Jennifer searched her mind for the right response. At a loss, she said, "You have a lovely home."

Sandy's face showed a mix of dismay and care. "Let me go make sure I have towels for you both for the morning."

15

Two Celebrities

The twin mattress squeaked whenever one of them shifted. Jennifer woke briefly in the night to find Chet's arm resting tentatively over her side. She pulled it in closer.

When she stirred again, it was morning and she was alone. She stretched then checked her phone.

There it was. A follow-up post on Tyson Brock's account.

Identified: The Antifa who attacked me is named Jennifer Soyvenus. She works at St. Mary's hospital. Call St. Mary's and tell them what you think of them hiring a violent criminal.

Fuck.

She scrolled through the comments. No mention of her address.

Her old address.

She checked some leftist accounts. Someone had posted a think piece: *Jennifer Soyvenus and the Limits of White Solidarity.*

She didn't read it. Instead, she found her bag and huddled away from the door, changing quickly.

When she came out, Chet was seated on the couch drinking coffee from a travel mug. He stood and asked if she wanted coffee then went to pour her some.

Jennifer heard Sandy appear in the kitchen and say something about making eggs, but he said they had to get back on the road. They had a quiet, almost tense discussion about where Chet and Jennifer were headed, which apparently was a cabin trip. Then Chet reappeared with a mug and offered it to her.

"Sleep okay?" he asked.

She nodded and smiled politely. "You?"

"Great."

It was 8 a.m. when they pulled onto the interstate.

"Didn't figure we should stay longer," Chet said. "I don't want to get them caught up in whatever situation we're in."

Jennifer nodded absently. "Your friend Tyson found out my name and posted it."

Chet let out a long, slow exhale. "Fuck."

"Yeah."

"Asshole."

"Yeah."

"Do you want me to go find him and kick his ass?"

She shook her head. "It was bound to happen."

"I'm sorry."

"It's okay," she said. "I don't want to think about it."

"Okay."

They sat in awkward silence for a while. Then Chet said, "My mom give you a tough time doing dishes?"

"No. She was nice."

Chet passed a semi-truck, keeping his eyes on the road. "What all did you talk about?"

"I told her you fucked the patriotism back into me," said Jennifer, tilting her head.

Chet scoffed. "No, you didn't."

"Boring stuff," said Jennifer. "Seattle. We didn't talk much."

"Hmm."

"Am I the first terrorist you've brought home to Mom and Dad?"

Chet grinned. "Would you be jealous if I said you weren't?"

"You know us Marxists. We don't mind sharing."

He chuckled. "I think you like being a fugitive. You get feisty."

Jennifer shrugged. Fugitive indeed. Her stomach twisted when she thought about it. Disowned by her friends as a traitor, rightly so maybe. Hitting the road with this right-winger. Meeting his parents, even. She'd never given much thought to the private lives of these people. Their families. What kind of cups they drank their coffee from.

Chet cleared his throat. "Are you hungry?"

"I could eat."

"Do you eat McDonald's?"

She'd eaten McDonald's before. It wasn't really her thing, but if she said no she would sound either stuck up or fanatical. "I eat McDonald's."

He grinned and gave her a side eye. "Really?"

She chuckled. "Yes."

Chet thought a moment. "If you can name one menu item, it's on me."

She paused, then said, "Cheeseburgers," with a sly smile.

Chet shook his head. "We'll find a Starbucks."

***

The sausage sandwich Chet got from the drive-through was better than he expected—seemed like real meat and tasted like the kind of thing a straight man would eat.

Jennifer got a cheese-and-fruit snack thing and didn't seem amused when he told her it wasn't a real breakfast, but she didn't seem annoyed, either. She did grin at him self-consciously when she ordered something with oat milk, so they must be getting along fine.

Maybe it was embarrassing she had seen his house. She seemed like one of those types whose parents had a big house in the suburbs of Seattle.

Hell, it was embarrassing he was running scared from a little podcast drama with her in tow. Antifa or not, she was still a woman, and he wasn't happy about looking scared or defeated in front of her.

There was a gas station next to the Starbucks. When they stopped to fill up, Jennifer popped in to use the restroom and asked if Chet wanted anything. He said no.

Two guys about their age were smoking out front of the building. As she walked inside, they watched her pass. One of them seemed to sense Chet's gaze and looked toward him. Chet fixed his attention on tapping his card and entering the pin.

He hadn't really brought a woman home to meet his parents since high school, though they'd met Anna once at a ballgame they all went to together.

Chet felt eyes on him and looked up. The guys were still watching him. One had on a black polo and shades. The other was tattooed and wearing a red T-shirt and black ballcap. He held eye contact and gave a small downward nod, then glanced at the store's front door and put the nozzle in the tank.

Chet hadn't been home in a couple years. His dad wasn't much for conversation and the last few times they all got together, he and his mom ended up talking politics and things got tense. She wasn't a liberal or anything, just more of an old-school Republican in denial about how both parties served the same masters.

The two men were walking toward him. He checked the counter on the pump. There was still a ways to go.

"Hey, not to be a bother," said the man in the shades. His palms were turned up and he had a grin on his face. "We thought we recognized you."

The guy in the red shirt had stopped a few steps back and was watching Chet like he was unsure of him.

Chet kept his face blank. The man with the shades came close enough he could see a tiny reflection of himself in them.

"I don't think so," Chet replied. "Just passing through." He felt his shoulder blades tighten. "You guys have a good day though, all right?"

The men looked at each other. The guy in the shades said, "You do that podcast, right? *Ripped for the Right?*" His posture was friendly enough, the other guy's was inscrutable. "Chet Beefwell, right? I love the show." He reached out a hand.

Chet took a beat to process then smiled and nodded. These guys weren't going to let it go and he should keep things friendly until he had Jennifer back in the car.

"Guilty as charged," Chet said, and shook the guy's hand. "More of a passion project. I bet you two are the only guys who have heard of me around here." He chuckled.

The guy in the red shirt grinned. "I don't know about that."

The bell above the gas station door chimed and Jennifer emerged.

"It's good how many people are waking up to what's going on in this country," said the man in the shades. "Your show is great. Connecting those dots."

The pump stopped. Chet thanked him as he took the nozzle out then screwed the gas cap back on.

The men turned toward Jennifer as she approached.

"Hello," said the man in the red shirt. His eyes flicked from Jennifer to Chet to Jennifer again.

It was hard to read Jennifer's face. She smiled politely. "Hi there."

"Well, I appreciate it, guys," Chet said. "We'd better get back on the road."

Jennifer looked at Chet, and he looked toward the passenger side door.

"Where you two lovebirds headed?" asked the man in the red shirt.

Chet focused on steadying his breath. "Friend's cabin," he said.

"Take care now," Jennifer said firmly. She opened the car door.

"I'm sorry. How rude of me," said the man in the shades. "I'm John." He took a step toward Jennifer and held out a hand.

She paused, then shook it.

Chet moved around the car to Jennifer's side and put out a hand. "John, was it?" He let a little bite into his voice. "You take care of yourself out here, all right?"

Jennifer got in the car and Chet closed the door behind her. He took a step toward John. The two held eye contact for a second as the other guy moved in closer.

Chet turned to him and extended his hand. "You were?"

"Christopher," replied the man in the red shirt.

Chet calmly made his way back to the driver's side. "Nice talkin' to you gentlemen."

John smiled and took a step back. "Nice meeting a celebrity."

As Chet opened the door, he thought he heard John add, "*Two* celebrities."

Chet started the car and pulled out of the station.

"That was not good," Jennifer said.

"No, it wasn't," said Chet. In his rearview mirror, he watched the two men slowly make their way to a black Ford Ranger with American flag mudflaps.

16

The Flock

Chet's "apolitical living hub" was definitely a fucking cult, Jennifer thought to herself as they found an unmarked turnoff, drove up a dirt road for what felt like too long, then reached a sprawling cottage surrounded by several yurts and a greenhouse.

They parked on a strip of gravel in front of the garden. Chet turned the engine off, then took a deep breath.

A cloud of dust was settling behind them. Sunlight flooded the field. It was an idyllic scene. Large trees swayed gently, crowding the yard.

A baldish white man draped in a beige robe emerged from the front door and studied them from the porch. He stood impossibly still, posture straight but gentle.

Jennifer watched the man a moment, then turned to Chet, who was watching her with raised eyebrows and a tentative grin. "Ready?" he asked.

Jennifer knocked her knee lightly against the car door, thinking, then nodded and unbuckled her seatbelt. "We should have backstories, right?"

Chet frowned. "Backstories?" He glanced again at the man on the porch. "I figure we just say as little as possible." Then he added, "Maybe avoid any SJW tirades."

Jennifer hated that term. She opened the door, stood, then bent and popped her head back in. "Are you gonna lose it if there's not an American flag in every room?"

Chet flashed her a confused-but-annoyed-anyway look as he got out of the car and waved to the man on the porch. "Hello there," he called. "I heard you're open to visitors. Is that right?"

The man smiled and beckoned them forth. He seemed to be about forty and had a Bluetooth earpiece in one ear. "We enjoy meeting new faces," he replied, voice gentle like an ASMR video come to life. "Is there a community member who invited you?"

Jennifer hesitated, then followed Chet to the porch steps.

"Your community served raw milk at a seminar I attended," Chet answered. He lingered on the top step of the porch. "Got to talking to some of them but didn't catch names."

Skepticism flashed across the man's face, then it settled into a polite smile. "Wonderful. What draws you to our space?"

Chet and Jennifer looked at each other, then Chet said, "We wanted to be somewhere less...noisy."

The man smiled. "This may be just the place for you, then. You're welcome to stay for dinner."

"Thank you. We'd love to," Chet said.

The man turned to Jennifer. "My name is Cedro, by the way." He opened the door and gestured for them to come inside. "Welcome to the Flock."

Jesus.

Jennifer stepped in slowly and felt the temperature drop.

The house smelled like steeped herbs and mildew, and the entryway was cluttered but curated with candles, crystals, and nature photography. A long hallway led to several sitting rooms crammed with donated furniture and coffee tables on the verge of collapse. Beanbag chairs were scattered across the floor, blocking walkways.

Two men were posted on a couch in one of the sitting rooms, draped in loose-fitting button-ups and harem pants, speaking in gentle voices. One of them—a man in his thirties with an unruly beard and quiet intensity in his eyes, scanned them briefly as they passed.

Jennifer nodded in greeting, then looked away.

Chet walked stiffly, head fixed straight ahead, even as his eyes darted around the space.

In the kitchen, Cedro gestured to the table. "Let's just ground ourselves before we settle logistics."

Jennifer cautiously pulled out a kitchen chair, hearing it screech against the wood floor, then took a tentative seat.

Chet sat as well, crossing his hands and resting them on the table.

Cedro gestured toward the sink. "Can I offer you tea or water?"

Chet shook his head. "No, thank you."

Cedro smiled across from them. "We welcome visitors to stay overnight for a few days. The visitor yurts are around back; I can show you later. Those who end up liking it here can explore becoming community members.

That involves pitching in with maintenance of the space, community meals, things like that. Have you done farmwork or gardening before?"

Jennifer shook her head.

"Most visitors do choose to stay. For those who don't, oftentimes it's because they didn't feel comfortable consenting to our community agreements: We really try not to subject each other to ideological boxes here. We respect one another's inherent autonomy. No violence—and that includes mental and spiritual violence, no unwanted touching."

Chet watched Cedro without blinking.

"Sounds good," said Jennifer, skeptical but not yet finding anything to suggest she couldn't sleep here for a night or two.

"We hate...spiritual violence," Chet said. "So that's good to hear."

Cedro chuckled warmly. "Well, I'm not sure we hate anything here."

***

The dinner table was long and handmade, with beeswax candles burning low in mismatched jars. The spread was colorful but defiant: quinoa studded with something pickled, beet foam, a kale salad dressed with oil and sunflower seeds. There was no meat and no grains that seemed too sure of themselves.

The table was crowded—about twenty people crammed tightly together, another fifteen lounged on couches and chairs nearby, devouring their food.

Chet chewed a beige cube of something spongy, trying not to gag.

The person next to him, a sunburned man wearing only loose pants and a mood ring, offered him a slice of what looked like a grey hotdog. "Seitan," the man explained. "You'll like it."

Aware of being watched, Chet made a noise that was neither agreement nor dissent.

Across the table, Jennifer was already in character.

"We both grew up in the Midwest," she said with ease, spooning beet foam onto her plate, "but lately, things have just been so dogmatic. So much arguing about politics and too many ads everywhere. We needed space to reconnect with ourselves."

The group murmured approvingly. Someone said, "Reconnection. Exactly."

Chet swallowed and wiped his mouth. "Good to unplug from all that mainstream media."

The room fell into an evaluative silence, broken only by the scraping of a fork against a plate.

Chet noticed some people were assessing him while others avoided eye contact.

Cedro, seated casually at the middle of the long end of the table, smiled warmly. "Well, no billboards here. Just trees."

A few folks laughed and Chet let out an unnatural chuckle.

A white woman with dreadlocks reached across the table and laid two fingers on Chet's forearm. "There's a lot to unplug from. The longer you're here, the more you'll realize you need to be."

Jennifer watched the exchange with a stoic face, then briefly looked at Chet.

Cedro cleared his throat and scanned the table. "This evening we'll be enjoying one of our favorite community bonding activities." He gazed meaningfully at Chet then Jennifer. "You're more than welcome to join us."

Chet started to accept politely, but Jennifer cut in to say they were tired from travel.

"Oh, you'd love this though," said the woman with the dreadlocks. She leaned across a few people to hold out a hand to Jennifer. "Really, you will."

Cedro smiled. "Your choice, of course."

Chet felt eyes on him. Before the silence could stretch too long, he asked, "What exactly will you be doing?"

Cedro gestured for the woman with dreadlocks to explain.

Jennifer shot Chet another look like she thought he could read her mind.

"Sharing time." The woman set her fork down as she spoke. "We call them Mental Freedom Sessions." She glanced at Cedro. The way she looked at him reminded Chet of how Roxy used to look at him. "We open up about the ways brainwashing has impacted our lives. It's nice to feel less alone. It gets to all of us."

The group mumbled in agreement. "It really is special," said a woman seated at the far end of the table.

To Chet, this all sounded extremely gay. He was hoping this place would be more into living off the land, making your own cold medicine out of herbs, chopping wood, hunting. That sort of thing. Still, they needed to get on well enough here for a few days while they figured out their next move. "Oh yeah," he said. "That sounds like a blast."

Jennifer stared at her plate, candlelight flickering across her face.

"We do them every day," Cedro said, gazing at Jennifer warmly. "So, if you're too tired tonight, you can join some other time."

An older man was watching Chet with patient intensity. "Have you two been affected by brainwashing?" he asked.

Chet glanced across the table at Jennifer, who seemed to be waking from a dream.

She sat forward in her chair and raised a mug of something lavender colored to her mouth. "Maybe," she said. "We all have, haven't we?"

Another pause.

"Have you been...fanatics about anything before?"

"Not really," Chet said quickly. "It was everyone else out there."

"They tried to put us in their boxes," added Jennifer. "It was very...wounding."

Another silence.

Cedro took a sip from his mug. "That's okay. You've come to the right place." He looked around contentedly as others nodded. "Wounds aren't real here."

The group turned back to their plates, relieved.

***

After dinner and cleanup, most of the group trickled into the meeting room for their Mental Freedom Session.

Chet asked if Jennifer wanted to go, but she'd said no and told him to go ahead without her. She found herself hiding away in a sitting room with several comfy couches, eclectic lamps, and a filthy Turkish rug.

She checked Tyson's post again. Comments were slowing. No major developments since he had announced her name. She took that as a good sign.

Her manager had consistently sent her texts just about every day since things blew up. Jennifer hadn't responded to any of them. The last one said: *I'm considering this a resignation at this point. Hope you're okay.*

She knew she should care about that, but she didn't. What she cared more about was that she hadn't heard from Marnie or Dev.

She found herself clicking onto Dev's Facebook. A new post was up.

New podcast episode out: "I Dated a Nazi (Unknowingly)."

Something in her twisted.

Was this fucking post about her?

This is maybe the hardest episode I've had to make. But I'm trying to be accountable. And vulnerable. By now, you've all heard that I recently discovered a person I dated once, who was still a close friend, was secretly a Nazi the whole time. As an ally, I know that as painful as this discovery was for me, it was even more painful for marginalized communities. And for that, I apologize. In this subscriber-exclusive, I reflect on why I missed the warning signs, how I can be a better ally, and what it means to heal from betrayal.

Jennifer zoned out amidst the smell of mildew and the faint glow of lamp lighting.

"I hope I'm not interrupting," Cedro said, announcing his presence from the doorway.

Jennifer pulled herself together and mustered a neutral expression. Shaking her head, she said, "I'm just decompressing a bit."

Cedro smiled approvingly. The floor creaked as he approached. "Reading anything interesting?"

The room was crammed with cluttered bookshelves. Nature photography, sacred geometry, New Age cookbooks.

Jennifer instinctively pressed the side button to lock her phone and placed it back in her pocket. "Just Twitter."

"I'll admit," said Cedro, "I've never been on there. Can you believe it?" He winced as if embarrassed by this.

Jennifer let out a polite, breathy laugh. "Probably for the best," she said. "I'm a bit jealous."

Cedro flashed a knowing smile. "You're welcome to use your phone as you please, but a lot of us end up giving ourselves permission to put them away. I'm only telling you so you aren't surprised when you don't see devices here often."

Jennifer pursed her lips. "Cool."

"Anyway, I just wanted to make sure you won't feel like you're intruding if you drop in on our group activity tonight. No pressure, I just like to check and make sure people know they're welcome."

This guy was a walking fucking red flag. She determined she could absolutely kick his ass if she needed to. It might be good for her to go and see what exactly she was getting herself into here, though. And it was probably better than sitting and stewing about Dev.

She took a deep breath, then slapped her hands on her thighs declaratively and stood. "You know what? I'll take you up on that."

***

The room looked like an odd crossover between an AA meeting in a church basement and a timeshare presentation.

The whole commune seemed to be crammed in there on folding chairs. Most of them silently waited; a few eyes darted to Jennifer and Cedro as they entered.

Chet was seated near the very back. There was an empty chair next to him—the only one left in the room. He smiled softly at her.

Cedro gestured for Jennifer to join Chet then drifted calmly toward the front of the room. He maintained a placid expression, greeting people with a slight nod as he went.

When she sat, Chet placed a hand on her knee and flashed a look of wide-eyed horror. She raised her eyebrows and nodded in agreement.

Two stools were positioned expectantly at the front of the room. Cedro perched on one of them. "Did we all have a good dinner?"

The room murmured a warm confirmation.

Cedro gave a sheepish grin and patted his belly gently. "I always overdo it on the seitan. Who cooked that?"

An older woman raised her hand tentatively and the man next to her gave her a playful shove.

"Marjorie, I should have known," Cedro said, grinning. He gestured toward his belly again. "Look what you're doing to me!"

The crowd laughed politely.

"I'm teasing, of course. Thank you to the dinner team tonight for nourishing our community." Cedro paused and raised a hand, extending his finger like he was waiting to make a point. "We have newcomers tonight, which we love. I hope you'll find a moment to introduce yourself and welcome them. Let me explain a bit about what we do in these Mental Freedom Sessions."

Jennifer leaned over to Chet and whispered, "Did you and your Nazi friends ever do group therapy like this?"

Chet chuckled but didn't attempt a comeback.

A woman in the row in front of them turned her head back toward them as if to look at them but stopped short.

"This is a place for us to explore and share about the brainwashing we've subjected ourselves to," Cedro continued. "This is not about shame or judgment. It's about self-discovery and knowing that everyone here has walked a similar path."

A man in front of Jennifer nodded.

"No one has to share, but everyone is welcome. Is there anyone who feels drawn to sharing tonight?"

The white woman with dreadlocks raised her hand, blushing.

Cedro beamed. "Yes, Nova, please." He leaned forward, hand outstretched, two fingers beckoning slowly.

Nova laughed nervously, then rose.

The man next to her flashed a thumbs up.

"Snaps for Nova," said Cedro, reaching out and touching her shoulder as she sat on the stool beside him.

The crowd snapped enthusiastically, and Nova shifted on the stool, smiling.

Chet looked at Jennifer nervously.

"Nova." Cedro bowed his head and closed his eyes. "Please, tell us your story."

***

After the session—which lasted an hour and never got any less mortify-ing—the man with the mood rings showed Chet and Jennifer to their yurt, which had a placard over the front door labeling it *Badger*.

The inside smelled like mildew and palo santo, and the hardwood floor was partially covered by a large, sheepskin rug.

They dropped their bags in the corner and fell onto the bed, exhausted.

Jennifer let out a sigh then rolled over to face Chet.

"Well, I told you the place was weird," he said.

"A man of his word."

The room was cloaked in serene stillness. The only sound came from out-side—the chirping of crickets.

Chet positioned himself on one elbow and brushed a lock of Jennifer's hair behind her ear. "It's a landing place for now."

"Yeah," she agreed. She moved in as if to kiss him but paused.

They remained silent a moment, looking into each other's eyes.

Then, she went for it.

17

Chicken Coop

"Will you be staying another night?" Cedro asked, holding out a cup of coffee to Jennifer. The rim was very close to her face. He smiled warmly, as if unaware he was too close.

Jennifer and Chet were perched at the kitchen table with three others. They had all been served a heaping plate of scrambled eggs by Marjorie.

Jennifer and Chet looked at each other. She narrowed her eyes and tilted her head slightly.

"We'd appreciate that," Chet replied, smiling at Cedro. He brought his mug to his lips and took a slow, loud sip.

Jennifer kept her eyes fixed on Chet. Her cheeks tightened. Something in his eagerness bothered her. He could have at least hedged and checked in with her first before saying they'd stay.

"Good," Cedro said. He straightened but didn't step back. "You'll notice after breakfast our community engages in our morning chores. You are welcome to participate or not. You can just wander around and enjoy the grounds if that calls to you more."

Chet looked at Jennifer. "Well, we want to earn our keep."

Jennifer pursed her lips. She needed to establish some ground rules with Chet—away from the watchful eyes of these lunatics. "Are there any good two person jobs?" she asked.

An amused expression flashed across Cedro's face. Then he scowled as if deep in thought. "Sure. But there are also some more team-oriented options with other community members..."

Chet started to speak, but Jennifer caught his eye and said, "What would the two person chore be?"

Cedro blinked slowly. "Have either of you ever cleaned a chicken coop?"

***

The commune had five chickens who roamed a humble, fenced area. "They're very friendly but they'll stay out of your hair while you work," Cedro explained. He gave them a quick tutorial—rake out the old bedding, compost it, sweep, lay the fresh bedding—then he made sure they had all the necessary supplies and departed with an overly-friendly "I'll leave you to it."

Chet shrugged, then picked up the two rakes and handed one to Jennifer.

Inside, the coop smelled like musk and straw. The chickens made their exit, clucking as the two fanned out and began raking out the bedding.

"Why did you tell Cedro we would stay another night?" Jennifer asked, carefully maneuvering around droppings.

Chet looked up. "Wasn't that the plan? Figured we'd stay here a few days and let things cool off out there."

"We haven't really agreed to a plan."

Chet stopped and studied Jennifer, biting his lip. "We sat in my car and talked about coming here, doesn't that count?"

The sound of rakes dragging across the ground would have been hypnotic if the two of them weren't bickering. "I just wish you'd held off 'til we could talk. I don't want to feel like a hostage here."

Chet dug his rake into the ground and swept hard, kicking up a cloud of dust. "I guess I'm confused. I wasn't trying to make you come with me. I thought we were getting out together."

Jennifer sighed. "I just don't want to be trapped here. I'm in a vulnerable position. You're the one with a car. I'm just...here. And I want to feel like I have a choice about it is all."

"Didn't you just have your name released online? What else is there to do, drive you back with a big nametag on?"

Jennifer planted her rake into the ground. "You won't control me with fear. I get to choose where I go."

"Jesus. That's not what I was doing."

She paused, watching him. She took a breath. "Then don't."

Chet's face was blank.

A chicken wandered cautiously back into the coop, keeping its distance but acting like it didn't see them.

Chet set his rake down and fished in his pocket for his keys. Then he took the car key off the chain, walked over to Jennifer, and held it out.

"What's this for?" she asked.

"Take it," he said. "I'm not trapping you here. I like you. We got ourselves into some trouble together. I thought this was the plan. You hold onto the key. You can go if you wanna go. I don't want you holding this against me."

Jennifer shook her head. "You don't have to—"

"Please," he said, extending the key again and catching her eye. "Just hold onto it."

Jennifer felt a mix of guilt and surprise twisting in her stomach. She accepted the key.

The chicken grew bold and sauntered up to them, clucking. It raised one foot, pausing with it in mid-air, tilting its head to the side then decided to take another step toward Chet. He smiled and bent to hold out a hand, but it veered away. He glanced at her sheepishly. "She doesn't like me much either, I guess. Must have gone to college, too."

Jennifer let out a breathy laugh. "I was just frustrated was all. I want us to make decisions together."

Chet bent to grab the rake again. "Heard." He popped out the door and reappeared with the wheelbarrow in tow. "We get to compost something," he said, stopping to pull on his gloves. "That should cheer you up, right?"

Jennifer rolled her eyes and put hers on, too.

As they loaded the wheelbarrow, Chet said, "I guess it was weird to take you to my parents'."

She shrugged. "This is *all* weird," she said, hunching over to gather more bedding. "I've never introduced my parents to any of my partners."

"No?"

Jennifer shook her head.

"No one notable enough?"

Notable. Was Chet notable? "There were a few. Maybe my parents weren't notable enough."

Chet glanced at her. "Why's that?"

She shrugged.

"So, you were never in love with that soy boy from the gym?"

"Dev? At one point, yes," she admitted, watching his face as she answered. "I was actually pretty broken up about it when we ended things on paper. Which was like a year ago."

"Really?"

"Yeah."

"Why did it end?"

"Well, when we were together, I think I felt...disappointed in him a lot," she said. "There's a certain type of guy in leftist spaces who says all the right things and looks the part but you can tell, deep down, they just want to fuck leftist women."

Chet raised his eyebrows. "I could have told you that."

She looked away, studying the distant snippet of garden that was visible through the coop's door. "I wasn't awesome either, though. I think I hurt his feelings a lot. Pushed him away. I'm hard on people."

A smile crossed Chet's face like he was about to make a joke, then his face fell. "I could see a guy like that being annoying."

"He could be. He could also be very sweet, though. And when he got really excited about polyamory, I was like, 'fine.' But then I realized he really wanted to end it with me. And then I was heartbroken. Like really, like what is wrong with me that I fucked this up?" She wiped her hands, looking down as bits of bedding fell to the ground. "But then we kept sleeping together and pretty soon I was sick of him again."

Chet let out a breath and rested his rake against the wall. "Loving people is...messy," he said, without looking up. "Complicated, I guess."

They began crossing the yard, with Chet pushing the wheelbarrow.

Jennifer cleared her throat. "What about you and Roxy Steele?"

"Roxy and I were only together six months."

"Did you love her?"

A beat. "Maybe," he answered.

"Maybe?"

Chet looked at her, then sighed. "No." He looked uncomfortable admitting that. "Not in the *love* love way. I liked her. Cared about her."

Jennifer blinked. "Why didn't you love her? She's kind of the female version of you, isn't she?"

Chet chuckled. "Maybe. Something about us never really clicked."

"Like what?"

Chet scrunched his face and his eyes tilted up like he was finding the words. "Like all the things I was excited about—the podcast, getting recognition in the Patriot movement—all of a sudden, she was so excited about them, and I just...wasn't anymore."

"Because she was into the same stuff?"

"Or because that was all she liked about me." Chet's face was blank and his voice flat. "And I thought, 'well, isn't there more to me?' And then I thought...'maybe there isn't.'"

The compost pile was massive—plant trimmings, litter from the coop, apple cores, and zucchini ends. Flies buzzed around lazily.

Jennifer watched him empty the wheelbarrow. Then she asked, "How was the sex?"

He didn't seem to love that question. "Jesus."

"I'm just asking. We've had sex. I'm not jealous, I just... It's just something people ask." Then, she quickly added, "You don't have to answer."

Chet was silent a moment, then asked, "How was sex with Dev?"

She'd never given it that much thought. "It was fine. Nothing mind-blowing. Familiar. We knew how to have sex with each other, you know? We'd explored a lot."

"'Explored a lot,'" Chet repeated, furrowing his brows. "Okay."

There was a hint of jealousy in his voice. What was this guy's sex life like beyond her? No way he and Roxy were engaging in the same stupid, political dirty talk. "What about you and Roxy? Was it good?"

Chet seemed like he was deciding whether to answer. "Sometimes it was good. Sometimes it was...great. But it was..." He trailed off.

"What?"

"Kind of the same thing over and over."

Interesting. "Monotonous?"

"I guess so," he said.

A light wind was moving through the trees, and somewhere a bird sang.

"You two didn't do much...exploring?"

He cleared his throat. "I think she had an idea of how conservatives have sex. Like, she even acted like we were playing a part when we were doing that."

Something about this conversation had quickened Jennifer's pulse. "What kind of things did you want to try that she didn't?"

He made a face and gazed straight ahead. "It doesn't matter."

They started making their way back to the coop.

"Have you ever been in love?" Jennifer asked.

Chet made a thinking sound, then nodded. He adjusted his grip and kept pushing.

"Who was she?"

"Her name was Anna."

"How'd you two meet?"

"I did an auto shop program at the community college. She was on a pre-nursing track."

Jennifer tilted her head and studied him. "You have a type."

"Maybe."

They were close to the coop now. The chickens had gathered near the door, a few came out clucking to greet them while the rest fled again.

"Was Anna a right-winger?"

"Neither of us were that political when we met. I think…she kinda went one way, and I kinda went the other." Chet paused at the entrance to the coop, took his gloves off and leaned against the wall. "She was taking these classes and going online and getting all worked up about 'gender roles.'" He glanced at Jennifer. "And then she started getting into…the whole LGBTQ thing." Chet prodded a bag of fresh bedding with his foot. "Broke up with me and moved to Austin. Started dating a woman."

"I'm sorry," she said, and leaned against the wall beside him.

"Yeah, well. Sometimes you lose people."

Jennifer saw Cedro approach the people in the garden. He stopped a few steps away from them, said something, and they laughed. He glanced briefly in their direction.

"How did you feel about the…gender role stuff?"

Chet shrugged. "It always sounded like liberal babble to me. Manhating. Our fights became less about things I did or said and more about who I was."

"Is that what got you into politics?"

Chet put his gloves back on. "I don't know. I guess I was spending more time online as things got weirder between us. And even more time online when she left." He walked back into the coop, and Jennifer followed. "I was hanging out at Tyler's gym, and we all had kinda similar backgrounds. Towns where the Democrats had decided to ship all the jobs somewhere else. We started recommending podcasts and forums to each other. And then COVID—" Chet's eyes darted toward Jennifer then away, and he focused on opening one of the bags.

There it was. Her fascination was quickly becoming regret. "Don't tell me you don't believe in COVID."

Chet didn't answer right away. He bit his lip. "I, uh—I lost my grandmother during that thing." He was kneeling at the bags, but he stopped working.

Jennifer watched him, unsure what to say. Then, she knelt beside him. "That really sucks. I'm sorry. Were you two close?"

"I lived with my grandma for about a year after my dad's accident. She was tough as nails. She had this walker she would rattle against the floor when I mouthed off. 'Don't lose your head with me.' I think I was pissed off a lot at that age, and she kept me in line."

"And she died of COVID?"

Chet shook his head. "She had a stroke and it wasn't her first. The doctors knew that was it for her. I went down to the hospital to sit with her but...lockdown. They wouldn't let me in. I said, 'I'll wear your fruity mask, just let me sit with this woman.' And they called security on me. This fucking asshole with his fake fucking uniform and his taser, hiding behind his stupid fucking mask. I almost decked him right there. I mean, I was *this* close to knocking the shit out of him. But then for some reason I thought, 'no, Grandma will know, and she'll be mad.' So I left and she died alone."

The chickens had returned and were circling them, curiously pecking at the bags of fresh bedding.

"That's spiritual violence," Chet said. "If you wanna talk about spiritual violence. Ripping someone's family away when it matters most."

Jennifer watched his shoulders rise and fall with each breath.

Chet cleared his throat. "I'm sorry. I shouldn't—"

"It's okay," Jennifer said. She rested her head on his shoulder.

"Well, anyway. It smells like shit in here."

Her neck was cramping, but she didn't move. "It does."

"What about you, then?" he asked, patting her foot. "How'd you get into left-wing terrorism?"

Jennifer kissed his neck and caught a flash of surprise in his eyes. "High school."

"High school?"

She walked her fingers along his leg. "Feminist punk and lefty zines. Then Junior year, this guy Todd had moved from New York, and he was cute, and he took me to anarchist book fairs and stuff."

"Jesus."

"And then Black Lives Matter. The early wave, 2015. Seattle cops kept killing people." Jennifer checked Chet's face, but it was unreadable. "Some bonehead asshole showed up at one of those things and punched Todd in the face. And we were...so scared. We were seventeen. And this woman showed up and got us away and helped patch him up. I hadn't thought about that in a while."

"Were your parents...into that stuff? Well, I mean, they were from Seattle."

"They didn't like the anticapitalist stuff. I was fighting with my dad a lot about his company."

"What kind of company?"

"I...I do come from money," she admitted. "I know that. That's not everyone on the left. But my dad worked for a venture capital firm. I kept learning all these horrible things about how they made money. Dismantling businesses. Laying off thousands of people."

"Fuckers." He checked her reaction. "Sorry."

"No, I agree. I would come home and confront him about it, and he would just shut down. Then my mom would scream her head off at me for it. 'Ungrateful.' 'Selfish.' 'How dare you?' And I was like, you two hate each other. You hate this man. And he treats you like shit. And you just...stand up for him? Anyway, I didn't really talk to them much senior year, and then I got into college and they paid my tuition and...that was really where things trailed off with us."

"You don't keep in touch?" Chet had pity in his eyes that made her feel...something. Smothered, maybe. Or embarrassed.

"Not really, no."

"I'm sorry."

Jennifer studied the coop, noticing for the first time how small it felt. "My decision, mostly. It's okay." She let out a sigh and then stood. "Let's get back to work. That's enough sob story."

Chet nodded and rose, too. He wasn't looking at her, and she realized he might think she meant his story about his grandmother.

"My story, I meant," she clarified.

Chet looked confused.

Jennifer cleared her throat. "I meant me."

18

Anarcho-Pussy

Her mouth was on his cock and it was awesome.

After another awkward lunch, followed by a Mental Freedom Session where Cedro made various commune members divulge beliefs they once held—Christianity, the Incel movement, a former KKK member, and a recovering vegan—the commune had dinner. After, Chet and Jennifer returned to their yurt.

Apparently, Jennifer had liked his whole pity party about his grandma, which made him feel better about it. Now he was lying on the bed with his pants half down, and the room was melting away.

Jennifer stopped and sat back on her heels. She looked up at him with those big blue eyes and he looked right back.

"Whatever you want me to say for you to keep going, I'll say it," he said, grinning.

She laughed and kissed it. "I was just wondering about something."

"What was that?"

She got on the bed and straddled him and he caught a whiff of her scent. His hand moved instinctively toward her waist and he fought the instinct to press himself into her.

"I was wondering what kind of things you had wanted to try that Roxy wouldn't try with you."

Chet felt his heart pick up pace. He slid his hand up the small of her back and swatted her ass. "Blackmailing me?"

"No..." She ran her hands over his chest and then pushed herself up and away from him. "It's just the curiosity has been...nagging me."

He was still rock hard and she was just barely pressing against him. Her underwear was on, but if he pressed in, he would bet she was wet enough to fuck her right there.

"What's nagging me right now is how much I want to be inside that anarchist pussy of yours."

She reached back to slide her panties to the side, pressing her fingertips against his shaft until his head was just against her. "*This* anarchist pussy?"

He was breathing heavily now. "Yeah."

She moved herself down until he could just barely feel her around his tip but stopped. Real wet.

His cock strained.

"I'm just saying," she said. "I can be quite adventurous."

"That right?"

She nodded and her breath fanned across his face and neck.

"Jesus, you feel good."

She moved back and let him in a bit deeper—still barely inside, but enough to send a shiver through him. "Maybe I would let you try those things with me."

He chuckled. "Now why would you do that?"

She slid forward so he was out of her again, made a mock thinking face, then said, "Because you gave me a car today."

He laughed and tugged her shirt over her head. "It was a while ago," he said, teasing her nipples. "It was a stupid idea. I just want to be inside you."

"You can tell me." Jennifer was crouching so that he pressed right up against her again, but not enough to let him in.

"I probably could."

"You probably could."

Chet pursed his lips. He wanted to run his mouth over her and fuck her until she was full of his cum. He had a warm, fuzzy feeling and he realized he'd already blown up his whole life and gotten all weepy in that chicken coop and if it meant trying something new—here, where no one else would ever know—he might as well. "Okay," he said. "Well..."

She thrust herself back once. He went deeper into her for a second and he almost whimpered.

"One time, I thought it would be interesting to...do the whole...role reversal thing."

She raised an eyebrow and smiled. "Role reversal?"

"You know..."

Jennifer dipped her mouth to his ear and whispered, "I do, but tell me more." She slid down on him again, slowly this time.

Chet's heart was so fast now it felt like it might burst. "I went out and bought a— Uh...a strap on for her to wear. Left it in a bag in my trunk. Discreet. And I asked her if she was into it. She said no, said that it was gross and everything, so that was that. Never even brought it in the house."

She kissed his neck. "She didn't wanna fuck you in that cute ass you've got?"

That did something to him. He thrust into her and she moaned.

"It was stupid." He kept thrusting into her, harder now, her hips bucking with each thrust.

"No, it wasn't."

"Yes, it was."

"Wait."

He stopped and watched her, panting, hungry for more.

Jennifer cocked her head. "Do you still have that thing in your trunk?"

***

At that afternoon's Mental Freedom Session, the KKK guy's name was Travis. He had short hair, watchful eyes, and was maybe in his mid-thirties, dressed in a flannel and jeans. He scanned the room warily.

"I was a member of the Ku Klux Klan for eight years," he began. "It was everything to me. All my friends were members. Got to the point where we never really hung out with people who weren't. Didn't even wanna hang out with the Whites who hung out Blacks and Mexicans, 'cause they were race traitors."

When they returned from the car, Jennifer pushed Chet back and crawled over him, dragging her nails up his thighs and sinking onto his face without preamble. Her pussy smothered his mouth, thighs clamped tight against his ears.

He moaned and licked.

She rocked against his tongue slowly. "You like worshipping anarcho-pussy?" Jennifer cooed.

He grunted, mouth open, tongue working.

Travis had said, "I think it was the first time I felt like I meant something. Like the world made sense." He looked down at his hands when he said that. "Like everything that was going wrong had an explanation now. Things in my life were bad because the people who ran things had this plan. They hated me. They wanted me gone. They were killing us off, slowly. Replacing us. Telling us we didn't matter. Trying to poison us. Erode us away 'til there was nothing left."

When Jennifer came, her entire body trembled. She dismounted, flipped him over, and began prepping him with care—spit, lube, fingers.

He flinched.

She paused. "Are you sure you want to try this?"

"Yes." He buried his face in the pillow, heat crawling up his neck.

Her fingertips probed him gently. His stomach muscles tensed, then relaxed. The sheet beneath him felt cool against his warm skin.

"You okay?" she asked, her voice gentler now. Her hands felt confident and safe.

"Yeah," he answered quickly. His breath caught in his throat. "Just...give me a second."

She stroked his back. That small gesture nearly broke him. His whole body was tight—not from pain, but from anticipation, shame, something else he couldn't name.

"Do you want to stop?" she asked.

"No. I want it. I just—fuck. I didn't know it would feel like this before anything even happened."

"Like what?"

He swallowed. "Like I'm about to go through a door in my house I didn't know was there."

Jennifer didn't say anything, just kissed the middle of his back and slid in a finger.

He groaned—half pain, half surrender.

She slid in a second finger.

He felt his anus loosen, contract, then loosen again. He let out another groan.

She paused. "We can stop here. It's okay to ease in with this sort of thing."

He shook his head. "I want to keep going."

A third finger. Deeper now, searching.

Chet felt like he might shit, then it passed. Blood rushed to his cock. He pressed back into her, letting her fingers in deeper, rocking back and forth as an uneasy pleasure rippled through his body.

"If you're ready, say you're ready," Jennifer instructed, "but don't lie to me."

Chet breathed deeply. "I'm ready."

Travis had said, "For a while it felt like I knew who I was." He'd glanced up at Cedro, who nodded encouragingly. "But then it started feeling like what used to make me feel powerful was just making me feel more scared. We were supposed to be scared of everyone. Mad at everyone. We'd start fights—sometimes other gangs, sometimes just normal people on the streets. It was really exhausting. My whole day revolved around being scared and angry. Then I'd walk around and see a Black family or a Mexican family or whatever, and they looked like a white family would look, just not white. And I'd have to remind myself I was at war with them. And eventually it just...wasn't making sense anymore."

Chet had scanned the room. Everyone was listening intently.

"I started to realize that the guys leading the group really didn't see me as me, either. They saw me as a soldier in this war they imagined. And they had imagined it so vividly...that I'd imagined it, too."

Jennifer strapped on the toy and pressed against him.

The stretch was deep, but the pain was manageable. What caught Chet off guard was the emotional flood that came with it. "Oh my god," he gasped into the pillow.

"You're doing so good," she whispered, sliding in another inch. "Just breathe."

The pain blended with pleasure. She fucked him slow at first, hands gripping his waist, thighs flexing with each thrust.

His body adapted and his breath evened out. Something in his core unclenched. The shame was still there, but it had softened.

Travis had said, "Nothing about me was better. The KKK hadn't made my life better. I was still broke and I was still lonely and I was so lost in it, like it was all I had left, but it wasn't...It wasn't anything. It wasn't fixing any of the stuff inside me. It wasn't even making sense anymore. It's so easy to just see the world around you through these ideas you have built up in your head. Sometimes you have to just set that aside and look at what's actually going on in front of you."

Chet had watched Travis intently, something odd stirring in him. Then, he'd noticed out of the corner of his eye that Jennifer was looking at him. Through him, maybe. Part of him had wanted to reach over and rub her back and the other part wanted to shove her out of her fucking chair just to make her stop looking at him like that.

When he started to beg, Jennifer picked up the pace. His back arched, mouth slack. "God, you're good," he moaned, the words tumbling out like a confession.

She reached around and slid her fingers over his cock. He was close. "You like being my little national security risk?" she growled.

He cried out.

"You like me fucking the freedom back into you?"

"God, yes."

When he came, it was messy, intense. His entire body shuddered.

Jennifer pulled out gingerly, rolled him over, and climbed on top. She slid onto his still-hard cock and rode him hard, still wearing the toy.

He gripped her hips, pressed the back of his head hard into the pillow, and bucked into her.

Jennifer leaned forward and spat into his mouth.

He swallowed without flinching.

She came loudly, then she collapsed on top of him.

They both lay there, panting.

His heartbeat was so loud, it seemed like the lights flickered with it. He rubbed her shoulder, slick with sweat, and started to laugh and she started laughing, too.

"Jesus," he said.

Her eyes fixed on his. "Yeah." She was smiling big. She was pretty like that. Eyelashes long, bangs matting her forehead.

Jennifer kissed him, then rested her cheek against his chest.

Chet pulled her closer and held on. He wanted to bury himself in her chest and never move again.

19
Mental Freedom Session

Chet felt Jennifer stir as the sun was rising. He blinked. A weak light filtered in around the edges of the blinds, and for a moment, he didn't know where he was.

Jennifer moved again. The blanket slipped off his foot and cold air hit his toes.

The sheets were clinging to their bodies, damp and wrinkled. Jennifer lifted her head, then flipped onto her back and stretched. Chet sat, letting his hand rest near her but not on her. She pulled the covers tighter and asked if he was feeling okay.

His stomach twisted up a bit when she asked that. He said he was fine.

She put a hand on his chest and asked if he was sore down there or any-thing and he grimaced. The thought of recapping what just happened between them somehow felt worse than doing it. He said he was fine again.

She was studying him now like she wanted him to say more. The back of his neck prickled. Those pretty eyes—looking through him almost. Sizing him up. For a moment, he wondered what would happen if he stood up and left the yurt.

"Okay," she said. She started rubbing his chest, then stopped abruptly and pulled her hand away. She glanced up and said something about how strange this place was and he agreed.

It was quiet for a moment, then she said, "That was nice though. It was very—it was nice."

"Yeah, we don't need to—" He let out a sigh and shook his head. "Let's just drop it."

She pursed her lips. "Okay," she said, then rolled over so her back was to him.

He wondered if he'd pissed her off and put a hand on her shoulder. It rested awkwardly, like he'd never touched a woman before. She didn't really respond, so he picked it up and ran it through his hair then dropped it to his side.

He *was* a bit sore, if he was honest with himself.

He cleared his throat and said again that this place was pretty weird and chuckled. She craned her neck to look at him and asked what he meant by that. Something in her tone startled him. He said, "This place. These people? Just...odd. Like you were saying."

Jennifer sat up and rested her chin on her knees. After listening to the prayer flags snapping in the wind for a long moment, she said, "Maybe we shouldn't have come here."

"This is just a landing pad," said Chet. "I thought things here would be...simpler than back home. Easier for us."

"Easier for us?"

Chet grimaced. She didn't want them to be an "us." Even after everything. "I just mean, no one here is doxxing us."

Jennifer massaged her legs with her hands, thinking, then asked whether they were good.

He scooted toward her but stopped himself. He said everything was fine. "I'm just saying, I'm sorry you don't like it here. I don't either. I was doing my best to get us somewhere safe." He let the silence hang for a moment, wondering if she hated being here with him. If she wanted to leave, where would she go? "You mentioned your parents are out there in Seattle. Why don't you...?"

Jennifer picked at the mattress cover. "I told you. We don't talk."

He cautiously asked her if they had hurt her or something.

Avoiding eye contact, she replied, "They just... All they care about is money and appearances." She checked his face and then turned away again. "And he hated her. And she hated him. And I wasn't allowed to be angry about any of it."

Chet grunted in a way that was supposed to sound like he was listening. He felt like he should say more but didn't know what.

Jennifer met his gaze. "Why do you say all that shit on your podcast? About communists, about the elites, about 'globalist infiltration.' Is that just trolling?"

That caught Chet off guard. For some reason, he put a hand on her knee. "No. Not a joke. Not really."

"Then what?"

Chet's chest felt tight. "People need to know what's happening...to how things should be. How they once were before things got all—"

"For white men?"

"Well, not just for white men. For all of us. And why not for white men? Don't we matter?"

Her mouth opened, then closed, then opened again. "Do you feel like you don't matter?"

Chet started to turn his chin as if to meet her eyes, then stopped. It felt like she had the upper hand after fucking him like she was the guy and now she wanted to embarrass him. "People like you don't think people like me matter."

A pause. Now he was getting heated.

"Chet—"

"You know, my dad worked in manufacturing for eighteen fucking years, fucked up his back for life, and they sent his job to Mexico and said good fucking luck. Make that make sense."

She didn't respond.

"My family lost everything." Chet shifted on the bed to face her. "And then I didn't do any better. And then all I got was shat on when I said it was bullshit what the Democrats were doing. Then I got into the forums. And I found out I wasn't stupid. And I wasn't an asshole. They were fucking all of us over. And that shit made sense. Those guys cared about me. And then suddenly, we were all Nazis just for saying anything about it."

When Jennifer finally spoke, she sounded angry but also like she didn't want to sound angry. "Who fucks over white men is richer white men."

The sunlight coming through the window was still faint. Tentative.

"It's your side, too. You hated us first. You and the elites. You protect them."

"No, *you* protect them," she said. "You're their boot on our neck."

"We're not allowed to talk about our jobs going away. We have to do everything the coastal elites want. If we say what we think, you call us racists or transphobes or whatever. Get us fired. Get us punished. The government forced us all inside at gunpoint for three years and you all didn't blink."

Jennifer scoffed. "Gunpoint? Give me a fucking break. You show up and support ICE. They're kidnapping innocent people *actually* at gunpoint. That's okay with you?"

Chet had moved himself to the edge of the bed. She was full of shit. "Maybe it doesn't matter what I think. You like thinking I'm a bad guy," he said. "That way you have a reason to scold me. Push me away. That's what you do, isn't it? With everyone."

Jennifer's mouth dropped. Her cheeks were flushed and her eyes full of venom. "So me telling you it's fucked up for masked thugs to kidnap people off our streets is about *my* issues? Fuck you, dude." She was on her knees now. "What about you? Your girlfriend thought you were gross for wanting to try anal. You people are fucking repressed and scared of everything."

He stood. "I'm not a bad fucking guy. You need to think I'm a bad guy 'cause otherwise you'd be scared shitless to fuck me. Isn't that right?"

She stood on the other side of the bed and started dressing. "You're so fucking obsessed with convincing me you're not a bad guy. I'm not your fucking podcast audience, dude." She walked to the door, facing him like he was a wild animal. "It's not my job to tell you who you are. Go look in a fucking mirror and tell yourself."

Then she was out the door, crossing the yard as sunlight flooded the room.

***

The sky was low and milky, like it hadn't committed yet to weather.

Some commune members were doing morning chores—a man ground something vigorously with a mortar and pestle, Marjorie hummed a song while she clipped herbs into a basket.

Jennifer found herself sitting on a bench near the garden, absently watching a snail make its way across a compost bin. If she wanted, she could squish it under her heel. The thought startled her.

This was the last place she had ever pictured herself—especially with a man like him. For a moment, she wondered whether her expulsion from her apartment was even real. It didn't feel like it.

She checked her phone to see if any of the posts about her had gained traction. Things seemed to have tapered in the last few days, which was a relief.

She scrolled local headlines.

U.S. Citizen Detained by ICE for Three Days Has Been Released

Suspected Immigration Enforcement Activity at Local Apartment Complex

Teacher Arrested for Interfering with ICE Operation at Local Elementary School

"There you are!" Cedro appeared, holding a steaming mug.

"Hello," said Jennifer. She didn't like Cedro's habit of appearing out of nowhere. Honestly, she didn't like his whole vibe. She'd watched him drift amongst the commune members seemingly casting a spell to make people do as he pleased, often without having to say a word.

"May I sit with you?" Cedro asked.

A bird call rang out, then settled.

Jennifer nodded reluctantly.

"We'll be having another Mental Freedom Session this morning," Cedro started, "and I was hoping you might be willing to share a bit about yourself."

A gate squeaked. Someone was feeding the chickens. They clucked and pecked.

"I don't know," Jennifer said after a moment. "I'm still not sure if this place is for me."

Cedro looked at her. "Of course it's for you. You're here."

Jennifer didn't reply. She checked for the snail again, but it was gone.

Cedro scooted in closer to Jennifer. "Can I tell you a secret?"

The back of Jennifer's neck prickled. "What's that?"

"Everyone who comes here—I mean everybody—is running away from something." Cedro studied Jennifer with soft curiosity. "I was. Everyone here was."

Jennifer could feel Cedro's eyes on her. She kept her gaze trained on the garden.

"What about you?" Cedro asked. "What are you running away from?"

Jennifer frowned, pondering the question and whether to answer it honestly. She was onto Cedro's bullshit, but she hadn't processed her recent life events with anyone except Chet. She opened her mouth, paused, then answered, "I blew up my whole life. My chosen family, my community. My best friend disowned me. I betrayed...everyone."

"Betrayed? That's a strong word," Cedro said. The lines around his eyes were tightening.

Marjorie's basket was full of herbs now. She stepped back inside the house through a side door. It squeaked shut behind her.

"I wasn't what...I wasn't what they wanted me to be," Jennifer said. "I wasn't...who I wanted me to be. I was lying to everyone. I felt like they were all lying about who they were, but then it turned out I was the biggest liar of all."

Cedro took a deep breath, then fixed his eyes on Jennifer and repeated the words back to her slowly. "You weren't what they wanted you to be."

They sat for a moment. A light breeze moved across their faces.

Jennifer caught a light whiff of palo santo and wondered where it was coming from.

"Something I like about this place," Cedro said, "Is that no one here wants or needs you to be anything." He raised an eyebrow and smiled. "We prefer to be nothing here. It's better that way. For everyone."

Jennifer squinted at him, then made her best attempt at a diplomatic tone as she asked, "What does that mean?"

Cedro laughed self-consciously. "Out there, people take sides. Build identities around them. It's all a trap. Happiness is impossible when you live like that."

Jennifer picked at a splinter in the bench. These people were just as indifferent to the suffering of others as Chet was. And yet here she was with all of them, no better. "Isn't that a kind of privilege?" Jennifer looked Cedro in the eye. "Opting out of everything?"

"Absolutely." Cedro smiled. "That's what makes it special."

Jennifer snorted. "There are real people out there. They have real identities. They hurt each other. They get harmed unjustly."

Cedro shrugged. "If you believe that is so, then it's so."

"That doesn't mean anything," said Jennifer. "You know that, right?"

For a moment, Jennifer saw a flash of what could be anger in Cedro's eyes. Then his face strained into a blank smile. "You feel like you're supposed to want to be out there. We all struggle with that. But at the end of the day, you came here. Why might that be?"

Jennifer let the silence sit for a while, then stood. "I'd better get back to the yurt."

Cedro stood and walked alongside her. "I'll walk you to the common space. It's almost time for the session."

"I'd better check with Chet," Jennifer said. Her skin crawled at his proximity.

Cedro smiled gently. "Chet's on his way, too."

***

Sunlight filled the room, catching specks of dust as they floated in the air. Folding chairs screeched against the floor as people found their seats.

Chet was standing by two empty chairs in the front row.

For a moment, she considered finding a seat elsewhere, but the room was filling quickly and the hurt in his eyes pulled her to him.

Cedro was up at the front on his stool, giving his spiel. Then he gestured to the empty stool beside him, searching the room expectantly. "Who can share with us today? Who here has been lost in ideology and wants to be found?" His eyes darted toward Jennifer.

Jennifer tried to shrink herself down. Chet's eyes were on her as well. A flash of rage. "Chet can," she said.

Chet's eyes went wide and he scoffed. "I don't know..."

Cedro had a bemused expression. "Chet, how wonderful. We would love to hear more from you."

Chet glanced at Jennifer, horrified, then turned back to Cedro. "I'm not very ideological..."

"Of course you are," said Jennifer. "Your podcast? *Ripped for the Right?* You're one of the most political people I know. Aren't you?"

Someone murmured behind them and Cedro held up a hand to silence the room. "I had no idea you had a podcast. Come, tell us more."

Chet was frozen for a moment, then he stood with a grunt. "It wasn't that big a thing," Chet said as he sat on the stool. "A lot of people have podcasts."

Cedro studied him, then glanced briefly at Jennifer. "Please, tell us about it."

Chet looked at Jennifer with pleading eyes.

That stirred something in her. "The podcast was all about how woke is destroying America. How the elites hate the white man and it's good when masked thugs round up immigrants at gunpoint. Isn't that right, Chet?"

The room erupted.

The dismay in his eyes made her want to throw up.

***

What the fuck was Jennifer doing?

Chet's skin crawled. He struggled to breathe as he looked out at the sea of eyes watching him.

The audience was chattering and Cedro looked panicked.

Shit. Rein it in. Fix it.

"It was more of a fitness podcast," Chet said.

Cedro waved a hand in the air. "Let's—let's let Chet do the talking here, please," he said. "Jennifer, we'll make sure you have a chance to share after."

Jennifer's eyes were fixed on him. Smug. Searing.

"Jennifer sharing is a great idea," Chet blurted, flinging an arm in her direction.

She flinched.

"She's even more political than I am. She's actually a high-ranking member of Antifa."

The crowd began buzzing again, and Jennifer glanced nervously around the room.

He felt his heart hammering in his chest.

Cedro's face was beet red. "Quiet, please!" He turned back to Chet. "Let's focus on you, Chet. How would you describe your podcast?"

Chet fought not to visibly shrink. "I told the truth how I saw it. I didn't like the left-wingers bullying everyday Americans. Making us feel like nothing. The podcast was my way to speak out."

Cedro nodded. "You felt like nothing."

He hadn't said that, had he?

Jennifer called out again. "And sometimes he and his podcaster friends would attack protesters and then post clips making it look like we started it." She turned around to address the room. "That's what happened to me, actually. Chet's friend called me a terrorist and then I got death threats."

Someone said, "Holy shit."

Cedro stood immediately. "Maybe that's enough sharing for now."

But Chet was standing, too, eyes locked on Jennifer. "This again? Tyson? I hate that asshole. He doxxed me, too." He pounded his chest as he said that. "Or is it more convenient to forget that? My friends want to fucking kill me 'cause of him. Because of us."

Jennifer's face was pinched "Why are they your friends, then?"

"You wanna talk about friends?" he asked. His voice quivered, but he couldn't stop. "Where are yours? They kicked you out of your own house. Disowned you. The 'tolerant left.'"

The room fell quiet. Jennifer looked like she might cry. He felt sick to his stomach.

Cedro put a hand on Chet's back. He looked like something had just made him very happy. "Thank you, Chet. A powerful story. You can sit down. Snaps for Chet."

The room erupted in snaps, like a slam poetry night gone terribly wrong.

What had he just done?

He stood and returned to his seat. His knee was throbbing. When he got to Jennifer, he started shaking his head to apologize and reached out to touch her.

She stepped to the center aisle, out of his reach.

Cedro extended his hand as if to touch her shoulder. "Jennifer, it sounds like you've been through so much. Would you please tell us about your recovery from Antifa?"

Chet wanted to punch him in the fucking mouth.

Jennifer dodged Cedro's touch, turned to the room, and scoffed. "No."

Cedro was frozen, hand still outstretched like something in his brain was glitching.

"I'm not recovering from Antifascism," Jennifer said. "I'm an Antifascist. That's who I am." She shot Chet a look. "And I'm getting the fuck out of here."

She stormed down the aisle and out into the hall, with Chet limping after her, calling her name.

20
Behind the Shed

Now Chet was studying the garden. All the plants these guys woke up early to water and trim.

He had given up on catching Jennifer before he reached the door but kept walking anyway. He looked back, half expecting the entire room to chase them off the property, but no one was there.

Chet headed toward the yurt. He'd blown his whole life up for her then watched her run off into the woods. Would she be okay out there? Honestly, she didn't need him. She hadn't needed him ever.

She'd have to come back eventually. Cedro and all them would be mad. Want them to leave. Jennifer had wanted to leave, too. But if the commune people tried to fuck with her, he'd beat the shit out of them.

Chet stepped on a patch of mud and let his shoes sink into it. He pulled his foot back out, feeling sluggish and weak.

He watched the chickens in their run in the distance. He was stupid to think coming out here could make things make sense.

She'd gotten mad then he'd gotten mad and he'd snapped into performance mode. It was the second time he'd thrown her under the bus for an audience, come to think of it.

He felt eyes on him and glanced back at the house. Cedro was in the doorway, watching. Chet turned away and kept moving.

When Chet reached the yurt, the lights were off and the smell of incense and sweat mingled. This was the only time he'd really smelled their two scents combined.

Their stuff was littered across the room. Clothing, toiletries, duffel bags split open—their moment together suspended in time.

He wished he could make Jennifer stay and work this stuff out, but there was no coming back from what happened in there. She wasn't the kind of woman to let up on this sort of thing. He had liked that about her, despite himself. Loved it, even.

Chet moved through the room, slowly packing. He'd pack her bag, too. It might be his last opportunity to be decent to her.

The strap-on lay on the floor at the foot of the bed. She'd split him open with it. But the problem wasn't that she'd entered him. The problem was that she was leaving him.

Now he felt like just another broken man from a long line of broken men.

He threw some of his things on the bed by his duffel bag and started gathering her stuff. His eyes stopped on her leggings lying on the floor. He thought of how they looked on her. How they hugged her thighs. Sometimes, when she was wearing them, he would want to drop to his knees and bite her calf.

He knelt, face buried in her leggings, her scent. He stayed there like that for a while, feeling his heart beating in his chest. Then he felt himself shaking. He realized then that his cheeks were wet.

Chet turned toward the door as if someone would be there. No one was.

He needed to stop crying and get it together before Jennifer returned. He began smacking his face to snap out of it, but the tears flowed.

He needed to stop crying like a bitch.

He balled his right hand into a fist and struck his cheek. His head lurched a bit and he choked on a sob.

Blood rushed to his head and his cheek burned, but it felt peaceful.

Maybe he was done.

To make sure, he clenched his left hand and drove it into his jaw.

He did nothing but breathe for a minute, face throbbing. He opened and closed his mouth a few times cautiously.

Standing, he wiped his cheeks and tucked her leggings into her bag.

***

Jennifer was in the woods, searching her mind for someone to call to get her out of here. No one came to mind.

She opened her phone to check her contacts. The screen was still on the headline: *Teacher Arrested for Interfering with ICE Operation at Local Elementary School.*

A terrible thought occurred to her. She clicked the article and read the first paragraph.

There it was. Leah's name.

She squeezed her eyes shut and opened them again. It was still there on her screen. *Leah Prescott.*

They'd taken Leah.

Jennifer paced. She read the article, mouthing the words.

ICE showed up at Leah's school to take a parent.

Leaves crunched underfoot. The smell of moss filled her nostrils.

Leah confronted them at the front desk. Filmed it. Refused to comply when they instructed her to stop. An agent struck her, tackled her to the ground.

Jennifer shivered, furious.

They'd taken Leah from her school.

She started dialing Leah's contact, then stopped. They might have Leah's phone. They might look into everyone who calls Leah. They might know about the video.

Her heart slammed against her chest. She wanted to sprint all the way home, find the fuckers who took Leah, and bash their faces in.

She shouldn't call her. She dialed Dev instead. Straight to voicemail.

She tried Marnie. It rang three times then went to voicemail.

Chet's key was in the yurt. She turned back toward the commune. Chet would have to let her go.

Some people were in the garden. She took the long way around to avoid them.

It wasn't right for Marnie to ignore her at a time like this. This was bigger than their fight. She couldn't shut her out like this.

Jennifer dialed again. It rang once.

Marnie picked up.

"You're not going to stop, are you?" Marnie's voice was cold, as if she was talking to a stranger.

"Is Leah okay?"

There was a pause on the other end of the line. For a moment, Jennifer wondered if Marnie knew. Then she heard a sigh. "They released her this morning."

Jennifer found a shed to hide behind. She knelt and felt the wetness of the grass against her knees. "Is there anything I can do? I can come home. I can do whatever she needs."

Silence. Jennifer wondered what Marnie was thinking now. She wished she could look her in the eyes.

"We're taking care of her. She'll be all right."

"I mean it," Jennifer urged. "Should I be there? Send money? Whatever I can do..."

"You're ridiculous," said Marnie.

Jennifer slumped down the wall. Her senses were muted—the dampness of the grass through the seat of her pants, the smell of mud. She was far away from home. And Marnie sounded like she hated her. "What?"

"This isn't about you," Marnie said.

Jennifer leaned back, resting her head against the rough shed siding. There was maybe a splinter in her back. "I don't think it is."

"Good," said Marnie. "Because you turned your back on us a long time ago."

"Marnie," Jennifer started, "I am sorry. For everything. I fucked up. I know it. But I care about you guys. And I need to be there for Leah."

"Well, you left us."

That didn't feel fair. "You kicked me out. While I was getting doxxed by fucking Nazis."

"We were in danger because you were *hanging out* with Nazis."

Jennifer gripped the phone harder. "You were my best friend, and you just *discarded* me."

"Do not make this my fault, Jenn. I asked you not to put me in this situation, and you didn't care because you don't fucking care about other people."

"Are you fucking kidding me?" Jennifer snapped. "I have always been there for you. Always. And nobody gave a shit about me, like ever."

Marnie was yelling now. Her voice in the receiver was garbled by static. "You. Fucked. A fucking. Nazi!"

Jennifer's throat clenched like a fist. "You're getting back at me. You're insecure."

"You're a fucking phony."

"You're just a fucking Twitter activist."

Marnie let out a slow, deep breath. "Where's Chet right now?"

"What?"

"You're with him somewhere," said Marnie. "Is that right?"

Jennifer glanced around as if confirming for herself, trying to find a way to explain and realizing how pitiful she was sitting here behind this shed.

"ICE is stepping up raids," Marnie said. "They're kidnapping, like, a lot of people. They pulled up to an apartment complex this morning and started rounding everyone up."

Jennifer put her phone on speaker and scrolled back through tabs. There it was: *Suspected Immigration Enforcement Activity at Local Apartment Complex.* She tapped it. It was published this morning, updated just an hour ago.

"They brought in fucking buses 'cause they're arresting so many of them," said Marnie. "And activists are going down there right now to stop it. Leah got out of jail and went right back out there. And where are you? Off getting railed at Camp Blood and Soil?"

There was nothing to say to that. Jennifer tightened her fingers around the phone. "I'm sorry, Marnie," she repeated. "Please tell Leah I'll do anything I can to help."

Marnie didn't say anything.

It occurred to Jennifer that the call had already ended. "I mean that," she said. "Please tell her." Then she hung up the phone.

Around her, the wind and the grass and the bugs carried on like nothing was happening. She sat there a while, staring at nothing in particular.

Then she turned her attention back to the screen. Scrolled Facebook. Calls for action online. Videos of tenants sitting on the curb, armed ICE agents checking papers. Activists arriving on the scene, trying to provide interpretation, legal observation. Some were gathering cars to attempt to blockade the buses.

This was a major moment where her community needed her. And where was she? Hours away with her red-pilled fuck buddy.

Jennifer watched a video of a young woman being dragged by two ICE agents onto one of the buses.

She watched it four times.

She wasn't scared of them with their guns and their masks and their vests. Not anymore. She'd already lost everyone.

Jennifer stood and walked briskly back to the yurt.

There was nothing left. She had nothing left to prove to anyone and she was free. She was free and she was a weapon now.

And she was going home.

And she was going to fight.

21

Yurt

Jennifer opened the door to the yurt and lingered. The lamps were off and the strip of light from the open door stretched across the bed. It was neatly made, its corners tucked tight under the mattress.

No sign of Chet.

Two packed duffel bags had been placed on the bed. She stepped closer and glanced at the bathroom door. It was pulled almost-closed, but in the crack of light, she saw his shadow.

Jennifer sank onto the bed and the mattress dipped beneath her. It had only been a few days, but the room already felt colored by their presence. The sheepskin rug, the hand-carved nightstand, the lamp in the corner with its crooked shade. The space was beautiful in its own way. Peaceful. She hadn't noticed that before.

The toilet flushed and Chet emerged, pausing in the doorway as if taking in the sight of her.

She almost rose but didn't.

He stood there awkwardly, like he wanted to draw closer, but his body wouldn't let him.

"Hey," he said.

She adjusted on the bed and folded her hands in her lap. "Hi."

He scanned her face, then averted his eyes. "I was worried you wouldn't come back."

She bit her lip. "I shouldn't have done that to you," she said. "I'm sorry."

Chet shrugged.

"I need to ask you to do something for me," Jennifer said.

Chet finally joined her on the bed. "Okay."

She studied him. "I need to go back. Will you take me?"

He nodded slowly. "I packed."

"Okay," she said. "Thanks."

Chet cleared his throat. "What does that mean for us?"

Jennifer traced a finger along the bedding. "I don't know. I—I'm not trying to be cruel. I just can't think clearly about this right now. My friend is in trouble. And I can't be...here, off with you while that's happening."

He was silent a moment. Then he looked at her and said, "I don't think we can go back and still..."

Outside, a gust of wind picked up. The yurt creaked.

"No," she said. "I don't think we can."

Chet breathed out through his nose. "What are you going back for?" He seemed accusatory now.

Her pulse quickened. "I told you," she said. "My friend is in trouble. I can't be here. I have to go back."

"So, this is nothing?"

This was almost what she had expected. A fight. Anger. Something. But he wasn't doing it how she'd pictured. Not scary. Not domineering or belittling. Just aching.

She sighed. "That's not what I'm saying. It *was*. It just can't be."

He was silent a moment, taking that in. "Do you feel like we could've made sense in a place like this?"

"I don't know," she said. "But if I stayed here, I wouldn't be me. And I'd hate you for it. And I don't want to do that."

Chet rested his hand on the mattress beside hers, brow furrowed. Finally, he said, "I can take you back."

She overlapped her hand with his.

"I'm sorry about all of this," Chet said. "I really am."

"Me too."

"What's happening with your friend?"

"ICE went to her school to arrest a parent. She got in the way and they took her, too."

"Jesus," Chet said. "They did that?"

"Yeah."

"Is she a citizen or…?"

She studied him, frowning. "Yes."

"And they still have her?"

Jennifer wondered if answering that truthfully would make him feel vindicated. "She's been released."

Chet raised his eyebrows. "Okay." He looked at her. "What does she need?"

"I don't know. She won't speak to me. None of them will."

He cleared his throat. "I'm not trying to scare you here, but it's dangerous for you to go back."

"Chet, ICE is rounding people up at an apartment building. People are blockading them to try to stop it. I want you to take me there. It's no more dangerous for me than it is for anyone else."

He shifted his weight on the bed.

"They're just people living their lives," Jennifer continued. She leaned into Chet. "And they're being rounded up. And I can't stand myself if I do nothing. I don't care if my friends won't talk to me. I don't care about Tyson. I don't care what happens to me anymore. Do you get that?"

Chet closed his eyes and took a deep breath. "I do."

She took his hand and stared at the sheepskin rug on the ground. It was splayed open, the wool fraying.

"I'm sorry about earlier," Chet said. "I'm sorry about all of that."

Jennifer swirled a finger around his knuckle. "This isn't about that," she said. "It really isn't."

Chet rested a hand on the inside of her thigh. "I guess I'm losing you, aren't I?"

"I think you are," she said. "I'm sorry."

He nodded. Then he said, "Can I hold you?"

Jennifer put a hand to his chest and rubbed it gently. "I'm sorry." She ran her hand up around his neck, leaned in, and buried her face in his cheek. "I don't think I have time."

22

Goggles

They drove in silence for most of the four hours, road empty for long stretches, tires whirring on the highway.

Chet clenched the steering wheel tightly. Every now and then, he'd glance at Jennifer, who mostly kept her head against the window, gazing out.

She checked her phone now and then. He asked for updates in as neutral a tone as he could manage.

The situation sounded like it was getting out of hand. Hundreds of activists arrived throughout the afternoon, flooding the parking lot and standing off with ICE and DHS agents. Local police had arrived on the scene as well but were not intervening.

They stopped once for gas. He put in just enough to get them back.

Jennifer checked the feeds again and gave more updates. Several TV news crews had arrived, plus some independent streamers. And some counter protesters. Their numbers were small in comparison, and they seemed to be keeping their distance from the point of conflict.

The sun was setting as they pulled into town.

About five blocks from the apartment complex, traffic was a nightmare. Traffic cops were stationed in front of barriers and redirecting cars.

Jennifer asked Chet to pull over and let her out. "You shouldn't drive any closer or they'll get your plates."

He was reluctant, but he pulled to the curb. "Maybe I'll walk you there," he suggested. "Make sure you get there safe."

Jennifer shook her head. "That's nice of you, but you don't have to do that. You shouldn't have to be seen with me."

Chet took a deep breath. He understood why she wouldn't want to show up to this sort of thing with a guy like him. But he wasn't sure he would see her again. "I'm not ashamed of you," he said.

Jennifer touched his cheek and he leaned into the warmth of her fingers. "It's okay. That's not what I meant." Her eyes dropped. "I've put you through enough today."

He took her hand in his and kissed it, probably keeping his lips there longer than he should.

"I'm sorry it didn't work out," Jennifer said, drawing her hand back and unbuckling her seatbelt. "I don't actually think you're a bad guy." She paused, keeping eye contact. "I just—I've hurt everyone I care about, including you. And I need to figure myself out. All I know right now is I have to do this."

He realized he'd looked down at the gear shift. He took a breath and made himself return her gaze. "Okay," he replied. "It's okay. I don't really know what I'm doing, either."

Jennifer opened the door, then stopped and reached over to hug him. Her scent filled his nostrils.

"Look—" He pulled away. "I'll have my car parked right here. I'm not gonna leave you with no way out."

She started shaking her head.

"You don't have to come back here," he continued, "but this is where I'll be."

She patted his hand, then stepped out of the car. "Bye," she said, then shut the door.

He watched her walk down the block until she disappeared. Nearby, a police cruiser jumped onto the sidewalk to pass the backed-up line of cars.

Chet scoured Twitter anxiously until he found a stream and joined. Then he realized it was Tyson's.

The parking lot was flooded with people. A solid group—probably fifty—had their arms linked around both buses. In front of the buses, more groups were huddled, some standing, some sitting on the concrete with arms linked. Others had brought lawn chairs.

DHS officers in full riot gear flanked the crowd. A handful of them were in a tug of war with a group of teens who were dragging cement blocks and folding chairs toward one of the exits to make a barricade.

Tyson surged forward to get a better viewpoint.

One cop struck a teen with his baton. Another raised his pellet gun.

A family passed Chet's car. A mom, a dad, and a boy holding a handmade sign. Chet forgot the stream for a moment and watched them until they were finally out of view.

***

When Jennifer came to the entrance of the parking lot, a circle of cops stood nearby. She cut a few steps to the right to pass them.

"Ma'am," one called.

She picked up her pace.

They started toward her.

The parking lot was loud with chatter and vehicle motors. Hundreds of people were scattered throughout the lot.

She pushed through the sticky heat until she got to where protesters sat linking arms to form a blockade. In front of them, a human chain was locked around each bus. They were holding hands through protective tubing.

Jennifer found a woman about her age and sat beside her. They linked arms.

"This is the Department of Homeland Security," a garbled voice on a megaphone said. "You are interfering with federal law enforcement and are subject to arrest. Leave now or you will be subject to further compliance measures."

"How many times have they made that announcement?" Jennifer asked.

"Two," the woman answered. "How many do they have to give?"

"Probably one more," Jennifer replied.

The woman was blonde, hair pulled into a ponytail. She had goggles that were a bit too big on her forehead.

"Or they won't," Jennifer added. "Sometimes they don't."

She felt the woman's arm trembling in hers and wanted to wrap both arms around her.

Agents in gas masks swarmed the bus, deploying tear gas. White plumes erupted and enveloped the protesters. Jennifer could hear coughing and screams and saw the outlines of bodies squirming.

Some protesters managed to break free and stumbled off, gasping for air. Others tried but couldn't.

"Shame! Shame! Shame!" the crowd chanted.

Someone sitting behind Jennifer stood and ran to the bus, replacing someone who'd left coughing. They were helping close the human chain again.

"I'm nervous," the woman said.

The police were closing in on Jennifer's group.

"That's okay," Jennifer said. "It's scary."

"This is your final warning," the agent with the megaphone announced.

"Have you done this before?" Jennifer asked, keeping her eyes on the cops as they raised their tear gas launchers.

"No, have you?"

"A couple of times, yeah." Jennifer looked at the woman. "If you get up and walk away now, that's okay. There's a crowd standing over there you can join. You can still be here for us. You don't have to get gassed."

The woman's voice was weak when she replied, "I'm okay."

"Hey, what's your name?"

"Lydia."

"Lydia, I'm Jennifer. I am going to sit here while they gas us. That is okay." Jennifer's ass was sore against the unforgiving concrete. The rumble of vehicles was almost deafening. She could smell Lydia sweating through her shirt. "You don't have to do this."

The cops were closing in. A few protesters scattered from the group. One of them tripped and two agents grabbed him.

"It's just your first time," Jennifer said gently. "There will be other times. We need you back here someday."

Someone behind them yelled, "Peaceful protest!" Others joined in as a call and response.

"Peaceful protest! Peaceful protest!"

A cop grabbed someone by the arm and started dragging them across the pavement. They let out a scream and their friend dove forward to intervene.

Lydia was crying now. She struggled to bring her sleeve up to her eyes and Jennifer released her arm and moved her own sleeve up to Lydia's face.

"Do you have friends here?" Jennifer asked.

"Over there," Lydia said, nodding in the direction of the nearby crowd.

"Go join them," Jennifer said. "Please."

Lydia stood cautiously. She took off her goggles and held them out.

Jennifer accepted them with a nod.

Lydia darted toward the safety of the nearby group.

Two agents trailed her half-heartedly.

A protester grabbed Lydia by the wrist and guided her deeper into the crowd.

Jennifer studied the goggles, turning them over in her hands. She put them on just as the first canister was launched.

***

Chet had been watching the stream for about twenty minutes. No sign of Jennifer on Tyson's footage, though it was hard to make out faces in the crowd, which seemed to be growing by the minute.

Almost none of the protesters were masked, and almost all were in every-day clothes instead of the fearsome all-black lefty uniform he was used to.

They were mostly just standing or sitting around. The most confrontational people were doing a big group hug around the bus.

The agents, on the other hand, were brutal. They turned their attention to a cluster of maybe twenty people sitting arm-in-arm.

The protesters just sat there while the cops yanked them and dragged them away or kicked them if they held on too hard.

Then, the agents started gassing them.

Chet felt his heart speed up as thick, white clouds enveloped the protesters. Half stood and fled, but ten remained seated, hacking and coughing. They writhed and covered their faces with shirts and handkerchiefs. Many had goggles on, and a few had N95 masks. He wondered if Jennifer was one of them.

Some protesters made their way to the group.

Agents shoved them from the side to discourage them.

The shouting on the stream grew louder. Some ICE agents had detained an old woman in a bathrobe and were leading her to the bus. She walked effortfully, leaning on a walker.

Her daughter and grandson, it appeared, were struggling to catch up to her, but several agents flanked them, pushing them back toward the apartment building. When the boy broke into a run, the agents chased after him. He'd almost reached his grandmother when an agent jumped and grabbed him. The agent fell backward. On his way down, he knocked into the old woman's walker and she tumbled to the ground.

Chet didn't realize he was getting out of his car until he heard the door slam behind him.

The jeers and shouting were already in earshot. They grew louder.

He passed one cop car, then another. An officer shouted from across the street and Chet picked up his pace.

Clouds of gas billowed around the lot. Flashlights and floodlights caught the motion of bodies in a murky, shifting haze.

One of the buses started its engine and the headlights flicked on. It blared its horn, barely audible over the shouting of the protesters and the garbled warnings of a cop on a megaphone.

The crowd erupted. Protesters flung themselves at the buses, wrapping around them.

He broke into a run.

About the Author

C. Lexcourt is the author of *The Patriot and the Antifa* and lives and works in the United States.